Was it a trap?

The air felt different, smelled different. Ethan hesitated a moment, then opened the door to the empty condo. The explosion shook the floor, shattered glass. Instinctively he threw his arms over Rebecca to protect her from the debris, as fire exploded inside the room.

"Bec, are you hurt?"

"I'm all right," she managed. "But what if...what if Jesse was in there?"

He pushed to his knees. "I'll find out." Fear darkened his eyes; then he turned and ran into the blazing condo, yelling Jesse's name.

Rebecca's heart clenched. Ethan would do anything for his son. She couldn't lose him or Jesse.

Heat seared her as she darted into the condo behind him. Flames clawed at the walls and filled her nose with smoke. Still she dug through the splintered wood. Her breath caught as she spotted something red beneath the mess. She dug it out and screamed in horror.

It was Jesse's baseball cap.

RITA HERRON

ANYTHING FOR HIS SON

HARLEQUIN®

TORONTO • NEW YORK • LONDON
AMSTERDAM • PARIS • SYDNEY • HAMBURG
STOCKHOLM • ATHENS • TOKYO • MILAN • MADRID
PRAGUE • WARSAW • BUDAPEST • AUCKLAND

Special thanks and acknowledgment are given to
Rita Herron for her contribution to
the LIGHTS OUT miniseries.

To Adam, my own son who I would do anything for.

ISBN-13: 978-0-373-88780-4
ISBN-10:   0-373-88780-9

ANYTHING FOR HIS SON

ABOUT THE AUTHOR

Award-winning author Rita Herron wrote her first book when she was twelve, but didn't think real people grew up to be writers. Now she writes so she doesn't have to get a *real* job. A former kindergarten teacher and workshop leader, she traded her storytelling for kids for romance, and writes romantic comedies and romantic suspense. She lives in Georgia with her own romantic hero and three kids. She loves to hear from readers so please write her at P.O. Box 921225, Norcross, GA 30092-1225, or visit her Web site at www.ritaherron.com.

Books by Rita Herron

HARLEQUIN INTRIGUE

741—WARRIOR'S MISSION
755—UNDERCOVER AVENGER*
790—MIDNIGHT DISCLOSURES*
810—THE MAN FROM FALCON RIDGE
861—MYSTERIOUS CIRCUMSTANCES*
892—VOWS OF VENGEANCE*
918—RETURN TO FALCON RIDGE
939—LOOK-ALIKE*
977—JUSTICE FOR A RANGER
1006—ANYTHING FOR HIS SON

*Nighthawk Island

CAST OF CHARACTERS

Ethan Matalon—This former Eclipse operative is about to lose it all—unless he can save his son from a sadistic kidnapper hell-bent on revenge.

Rebecca Matalon—Her son is missing, and the only man who can save him is his father—the man she once loved, but now is about to divorce.

Jesse Matalon—The five-year-old son of Ethan and Rebecca.

Ty Jones—Eclipse operative who discovers that the kidnapping is part of a much bigger plan to bomb Boston.

Liam Shea—The mastermind behind the revenge scheme against the Eclipse team, he's targeting them one by one and has a grand finale planned that will rock the city.

Finn Shea—Liam's son used Rebecca to get close to her son, and will do anything to destroy the man who betrayed his father.

Grant Davis—The vice president is still missing. Will the team find him in time to save his life and keep the Sheas from blowing up the city?

Prologue

Seventeen hours into the blackout.

Finn Shea smiled as the afternoon temperature in the city began to climb. People were frantic. Traffic jams clogged the streets; subways were stranded. A half-million people were without power. Businesses had closed or were trying to run on auxiliary sources. Tempers had flared and violence had broken out, escalating crime.

His father, Liam, had set his plan in motion last night, now it was in full swing. The target—the men who once belonged to a select coterie of Special Forces servicemen. The so-called band of brothers had performed highly classified, highly dangerous missions for the military, all flawlessly.

Except for their last.

Ten years ago their mission had been to rescue hostages in civil war-torn Barik, a small Middle Eastern nation.

A mission that ended his father's brilliant career.

And ruined his life.

Now his father was out of jail, back in control. And ready to mete out punishments to the men who had betrayed him and stood idly by while he alone took the fall for the disastrous mission.

Tom Bradley, who had been in command of the mission, was dead now. But the other six men had moved on, had lived good lives while his father had suffered.

Shane Peters, security expert. Chase Vickers, engine expert. Ethan Matalon, computer ace. Ty Jones, demolitions man. The only non-American, Frederick LeBron, a language specialist and a prince from the tiny alpine nation of Beau Pays. And last but not least, Grant

Davis, then the tactical expert—now the damn vice-president.

Thanks to his brothers, Finn knew actions had already been taken against Shane Peters and Chase Vickers. As for Vice-President Davis…well, Finn knew he'd soon come to an explosive end. Ethan Matalon was next on the hit list. Finn's target.

Yes, his father was finally exacting his revenge.

Because Liam Shea had been innocent. Nevertheless he'd been court-martialed, dishonorably discharged and incarcerated anyway. And his family's life had been destroyed. His wife had filed for divorce. Hoping to escape the publicity and shame, she'd dragged her sons from their Massachusetts home to that god-awful small town in Oregon.

But they hadn't escaped at all. Liam had been tormented every day in prison. And Finn and his brothers had paid the price, as well.

Liam's team was to blame.

And now each of them had to face the consequences.

Finn stared at the photo of Ethan Matalon's

son, Jesse. Five years old. Without a full-time father. Scared of the dark.

Finn forced a steel wall around his heart. He couldn't care about the kid. Wars caused casualties, he reminded himself.

And Ethan's Achilles' heel was his son.

It was only fair. Finn's father had lost years with his boys. Now Ethan would lose his own, too.

And his pain would be their revenge.

Chapter One

Jesse hated the dark.

Rebecca Matalon had learned to hate it, too. Her five-year-old son's cry in the night had woken her the evening before, and she'd spent hours trying to convince him that no monsters lurked in the shadows.

The insufferable sudden blackout that had hit Boston last night had continued into the day. So had Jesse's crankiness.

She stared outside through the fifth-story window of the Ritz-Carlton, stunned that it was already 2:00 p.m. and the power still had not been restored. Never had she seen the city such a madhouse of chaos and ill tempers. Useless air conditioners, accidents due to nonfunctioning traffic lights and vandalism had turned normal decent people into irritable, aggressive, paranoid, violent citizens.

If she were in L.A., she'd be at work reporting the mess.

Instead, she was trying to keep her five-year-old son entertained and happy without the joys of television, electronic games...or his father.

Ethan hadn't even been able to go to the Red Sox game with her and Jesse yesterday. And Ethan and Jesse's common love of baseball had assured her they'd always remain close.

In spite of the fact that she'd moved thousands of miles away.

She dressed in the coolest linen skirt and cotton blouse she'd packed, swept her long blond hair into a chignon and clipped silver loops in her ears. A simple assessment in the mirror assured her that she looked fine. Not that she was primping for this dreaded rendezvous with Ethan, her soon-to-be-ex, but she hated to face him looking like a bedraggled sleep-deprived maniac. After all, she was the mother of his child and had been his lover.

And they had had a solid marriage once. Truth be known, they still remained friends. They just couldn't live together.

Memories assaulted her, launching her back to a time when they'd first met. They'd shared an instant attraction, fallen in love overnight and married a year before he'd enlisted in the military. She'd survived the separation, but when he'd returned he'd been wrapped up in building his now-megamillion-dollar computer software company. On top of that was the covert work he did for Eclipse. Secret missions that he couldn't talk about. Dangerous jobs that sent him all over the world. She'd never quite known if he'd come home dead or alive.

Her heart raced at the realization that she had liked that dark, dangerous side of Ethan. The mystery, excitement, suspense had been a turn-on. But it was no way for a family to live.

Besides, she'd put her own career aspirations on hold for too long. After having Jesse and practically raising him alone, then working in menial jobs, she hadn't been able to turn down the L.A. job. A TV journalist—her life's dream.

In a bicoastal marriage, she and Ethan had drifted apart till she'd filed for divorce.

Now it was time to sign the damn papers and finalize the end of their marriage.

"Mommy?"

Rebecca's heart squeezed at the sight of Jesse's big brown eyes staring up at her. Ethan's eyes.

Could she really do this today—sign those long-awaited papers and put Ethan out of their lives for good?

No, Ethan would always be a part of Jesse's life. Just not hers.

"I'm hot." Jesse shoved his hand through his short blond hair, which was sticking out in a thousand directions. In his other hand, he held the glow-in-the-dark lighted wand that she'd bought him at the ballgame. Jesse had held on to it for dear life during the night, using it for light when he'd awakened in the dark.

"I know, sweetie. Maybe the electricity will be restored soon."

"I don't wanna stay in the hotel anymore. I wanna go play."

Rebecca knelt in front of her son. She hadn't explained about her meeting with

Ethan yet, but eventually she'd have to. Jesse would be upset. Apparently half the kids at school came from divorced homes, and Jesse had already announced quite vehemently that he didn't want to be one of them.

His declaration had broken her heart.

"Tell you what." She took his hand and guided him to the window, then lifted him so he could see outside. "See over there in Boston Common. That's Frog Pond. There are a lot of kids out there. Would you like for Miss DeeDee to take you wading in the pond while I'm at my meeting?"

"Uh-huh." He bobbed his head up and down, and she gave him a hug. Outdoor exercise would do him good. Maybe put him in a better mood and help him expend some of his restless energy.

She had to tell him the truth when she returned. She just prayed that one day he'd forgive her for tearing apart their family.

THE PAST NIGHT AND MORNING had been a virtual nightmare.

Ethan Matalon let himself into his prized

Beacon Hill brownstone, wiping sweat from his brow and cursing the damn blackout that plagued the city.

At 9:00 p.m. the night before, life as Bostonians knew it had crashed to a halt. Then chaos had reigned.

Ethan had spent countless hours fending panicked calls about the problems with security systems related to computer software he had designed. Major businesses and high-end clients who felt unprotected without the modern edge of technology to keep the evil-doers at bay had turned to him in their hour—*hours*—of need and he had done his best to comply. His technical skills had earned him millions of dollars, and helped him reach the pinnacle of success he enjoyed today.

Only that money didn't keep him warm at night. And it certainly didn't assuage the pain of knowing that he'd failed at other areas in his life.

He glanced at his watch and cursed. At least work had distracted him from his meeting today. The one he'd stalled for the past two years.

The one with his wife.

His *estranged* wife. Rebecca. The one woman he'd loved with all his heart. The one he'd married in good faith. The mother of his child.

The woman who'd finally called and insisted that they meet to sign the divorce papers.

Pain knifed through his chest, and he climbed the plush carpeted steps to his bedroom, his breathing labored. Closing his eyes to shut out the image of his son's small face and the disappointment that had shadowed his eyes the last time they'd spent the weekend together and he'd said goodbye at the airport, Ethan shucked his sweaty clothes and jumped into the shower. The cold water revived him physically, but mentally he was a damn basket case.

Five years ago, he thought he'd finally overcome the haunting remnants of his past, of his childhood. He'd believed he had it all. A beautiful wife who loved him. A new son. Fortune. The prestigious address in Beacon Hill he'd always dreamed of. And the hottest company in the United States.

Then Rebecca had left him.

He scrubbed his body, wishing he could wash away the memories of their time together. But they were embedded as firmly in his head as her touch was imprinted on his body. He pictured Rebecca smiling and laughing when they'd gone sailing in the harbor. Her golden skin glowing with water droplets when they'd skinny-dipped in the bay. The graceful way she'd moved like a ballerina when they had danced in the moonlight. The smile lighting her eyes the night he'd proposed. The romantic honeymoon in Nepal.

Rebecca's silky honey-blond hair spread across his chest. Her sultry hazel eyes, eyes that turned smoky when they made love. And those mile-long legs wrapped around his waist.

His body hardened with desire at the mere thought, and he cursed again. How the hell was he supposed to get through this meeting today? How was he supposed to get over her?

And why now, after two years of separation, was she insisting on this meeting? Determined to finally sever their marriage?

Suddenly, the grim possibility that she'd met someone else, that she was ready to move on, that another man had ensconced himself in her life, and maybe in her bed, hit him like a fist to his gut.

He leaned against the counter and stared into the mirror at his bloodshot eyes. He'd always known the possibility existed that she'd find someone else, but he'd shoved the thought into the back of his mind, choosing to live in denial.

Today he had to drag his head out of the sand and face reality. Rebecca was not only devastatingly beautiful and sexy, but interesting and damn smart. And her job as a TV journalist certainly had given her exposure across the U.S. Half the men in the world probably ogled her from their living room while she reported the news.

So whom had she met? Who had interested her enough to make her insist on finalizing the divorce?

Someone from TV? Another journalist? Some L.A. producer who'd swept her off her feet? Or maybe a Hollywood star?

He groaned and forced himself to dress. She would probably be waiting when he arrived at the Ritz-Carlton for their meeting. Would she be alone? Or would her lover accompany her? Would they sip champagne afterward and celebrate the end of him, and the beginning of *them?*

He balled his hands into fists and had to bite down on one to keep from slamming it into the mirror and breaking the glass.

If she had found someone else, what did his son think?

A choking sound erupted from deep inside him. The thought of losing Rebecca hurt. But he would handle it. After all, he'd grown accustomed to being alone the past two years. His business and the missions he did for Eclipse kept him occupied. He had a full life.

Dammit. He *did*.

But the thought of another man playing father to Jesse nearly drove him to his knees.

REBECCA WAVED TO JESSE AS HE slipped his hand into DeeDee's. The young nanny had worked for her for six months now, and seemed responsible and appeared to genuinely care for Jesse.

Sometimes she felt bad for the time she spent away from her son and for leaving him with a nanny, but a single mother had to have help.

A *single* mother. Ethan would say that she'd chosen the role.

But that wasn't entirely true. Hadn't she been alone before she and Ethan had actually parted?

It wasn't as if she'd gotten involved with another man right away, either. She'd only wanted to pursue her career, and take advantage of the opportunity she'd been given in L.A.

Jesse waved the small wand in the air as if it were magic. "Bye, Mommy."

She gave him a peck on the cheek. "Have fun at the pond, Jesse. Later, um…your dad may come over." Now, why had she said that? This trip was supposed to be quick. Sign the papers. Accept that their relationship was over.

Move on.

But Ethan had a right to see Jesse. And she

would never deny him that right. Or deny Jesse time with his father.

Jesse's big brown eyes lit up with hope. "Really?"

"Sure, honey."

He perked up and skipped toward the door with a grin. DeeDee waved as the two of them bustled out the hotel door. Rebecca waited until they'd left, then applied lipstick, grabbed the divorce papers and her purse and headed to the elevator. A couple stepped from the stairwell, reminding her that the elevator was out, so she inhaled a deep breath, then took the stairs. Five flights. Thank goodness she worked out regularly.

Due to the blackout, though, the stately hotel was hot, filled with complaining customers and not running at its normal model of efficiency. The dark stairwell was claustrophobic and suffocating. When she exited and made her way to the salon, where she'd asked Ethan to meet her, her legs felt heavy and weighted.

Exhaustion from the sleepless night added

to the fatigue. A case of nerves clutched her stomach in a viselike grip.

Everybody experienced a case of jitters before the wedding. It only seemed right that an anxiety attack would strike before the divorce.

Thankfully, the salon was empty when she entered, giving her a brief reprieve. In an effort to calm herself, she studied the fabulous brocade wall coverings, the striped damask wingback chairs, the intimate seating areas meant to invite conversation. It was a beautiful, peaceful place, one that held no sentimental meaning for them so she didn't have to be haunted by memories of the two of them reclining in front of the fireplace or cuddled together sipping sherry on one of the loveseats.

She sensed Ethan had arrived before she even pivoted toward the door. His masculine scent permeated the room, and she felt his dark eyes skating over her, making her skin burn with need.

Shaken already, she turned to face him.

He looked massive and intimidating, mysterious and dark, a man who stood out in a crowd. A man who took control. A man who lived on the edge. One who snuck away in the night to save the innocent with no regard for his own life. Born with an adventurous soul, Ethan led others in the fight against terrorism and evil.

And he loved his son fiercely.

She remembered the tears glinting in his eyes when Jesse was born. At the memory, emotions crowded her chest, led by a sudden rush of affection she hadn't expected to feel.

"Rebecca?"

His gruff voice sent a tingle down her spine.

"Hello, Ethan." Her throat barely worked. Her dry hands itched to touch him, to pull him to her once more. To kiss him hello.

To kiss him goodbye.

To stop this madness they'd started two years ago.

Heat suffused the room, the tension palpable as he moved toward her, like a panther stalking his prey. His dark look consumed her. Resurrected memories of erotic touches and whispered promises long into the night. Of lovemaking and marriage vows and total possession of body, mind and soul.

Of being a couple and a family. Of wanting their marriage to last.

But there had been so many nights alone.

"We missed you at the Red Sox game." Darn it. She hadn't meant to say *we*.

"I wish I could have been there. I…hate to disappoint Jesse."

Jesse. Always Jesse. But what about her?

Guilt tugged at her. She had to put Jesse first and forget about her selfish needs. She hated to hurt their son. And they were both letting him down now, taking the easy way out.

But really, their marriage had ended some time ago.

And now she had the possibility of someone else in her life. In their lives. Someone in L.A. Someone stable. A man who'd taken enough interest in Jesse to volunteer to be his Little League coach.

Ethan couldn't even make a Sox game on the rare occasion when she and Jesse flew to Boston.

"Is Jesse okay?" Ethan asked.

She nodded. "A little grumpy from the heat. He didn't sleep well last night."

A pained look crossed Ethan's face. "Still afraid of the dark?"

"Yes. He thinks monsters are hiding in the corners." Her voice wavered. "I tried to convince him there aren't."

"I'm sorry…" His voice trailed off, but his words held a wealth of meaning, and she knew he meant it to be a blanket apology.

She had to cut him a break. Ethan never meant to disappoint or hurt them. He had important work, was almost obsessive about achieving success, and was driven by the pain of his childhood. A pain he refused to speak of or share. Maybe if he had, they wouldn't be here now; they'd still be together. "I guess the blackout created a multitude of problems for you."

He gave a clipped nod. "I spent all night doing damage control."

Instead of comforting their son. Or her.

She didn't want to blame him anymore. Ethan was who he was. His work ethic was one thing that had attracted her to him. She admired his commitment to his software company, as well as his work for Eclipse.

It was time to move on for all of them. Better not to drag out the inevitable. She and Ethan could be friends for their son's sake. But anything else… The chemistry, the heat, the sex had always been explosive, but it wasn't enough to sustain them for life.

Sucking in a sharp breath, she removed the divorce papers from her purse and spread them on a table. Ethan's dark eyes met hers, turmoil clouding the depths.

She would survive this day and the divorce. And so would Jesse.

Then they could all go on with their lives.

IT WAS TIME TO TAKE THE BOY.

Finn's mouth watered as he watched Jesse Matalon approach Frog Pond, intent on wading in the water. Child's play.

Finn didn't remember ever being a child.

All he remembered was the pain of his father's arrest. The shame. The move. The bitterness. The need for justice and revenge.

He studied the crowd of people hovering

nearby. Mothers and fathers who'd left work for the day to venture outside in the light. Babysitters and nannies of Boston's elite who talked among themselves. Teenagers who strolled hand in hand, grateful for the summer break and unconcerned about who saw them making out in public or sneaking a smoke.

Jesse kicked off his shoes and jumped in to play chase in the water with the other kids as if he'd been penned up for days. He was a precocious kid who Finn might have liked had he not belonged to the enemy.

The nanny was distracted. Rebecca was nowhere to be found. Off to meet Ethan, the man who'd let her down.

Rebecca was such a babe. He wanted her, too, wished he could kidnap them both. It would be double torture for Ethan to know that his former wife had been in Finn's bed.

But kidnapping her didn't fit into the plan right now. And he had to stick to the plan with no variations. Variations might mean mistakes, and Finn couldn't fail. He'd waited too long for this moment.

Hell, six months ago, he'd moved to L.A.

to ingratiate himself into Rebecca's life. First, he'd set in waiting for his father to implement his plan. But he'd finally grown impatient and had orchestrated his own meeting. He'd come on to Rebecca, and she'd responded with interest, although she'd initially turned down his request.

But in time he would have seduced her.

Pity now that he wouldn't get to bed her. He had to take care of the kid.

Tugging his own ball cap down over his head to hide his face, he slipped through the crowd. Jesse would never see him coming, and neither would the nanny or anyone else. There were too many people in the park, too many distractions.

All he had to do was make his move, and Jesse was his.

Chapter Two

Ethan had taken out terrorists worldwide, maneuvered his way in and out of life-and-death situations that would make some people's hair curl and had nearly died of gunshot wounds twice.

But Rebecca still had a way of robbing the air from his lungs. Just the sight of her made him feel as if he'd stepped onto a landmine. His heart was racing, his palms were sweaty and the blood rushed to his head.

In spite of the heat and the sleepless night she'd obviously spent, she looked gorgeous today, light and airy in her pale clothing with her sun-kissed skin glowing from the L.A. weather, and her silky hair lifted off her neck. Normally he preferred her hair down, flowing around her shoulders, so the up-do should have put him off. Instead he appreciated the tantalizing view of the sensitive spot behind her ear that he liked to kiss. The spot that drove her wild and turned her into putty in his hands.

His lips puckered at the mere thought, and he almost forgot why they were there and dropped a juicy one on her neck. But the sound of papers crinkling as she spread them on the table jarred him back to reality.

His feet felt like lead weights as he forced himself to cross the room. He had survived countless dangerous missions—he could certainly sign divorce papers. After all, his marriage to Rebecca hadn't been a real marriage in over two years. He was an adult. Life had to go on.

"You seem in a hurry to get this over with," he said in a gruff voice.

Her startled gaze swung back to him. "In a hurry? Ethan, I moved to L.A. two years ago."

He sucked in a sharp breath. "So why today?"

Eyes narrowed, she chewed on her

bottom lip and glanced at the window, avoiding eye contact.

His lungs tightened. "You're involved with someone else?"

Tension rattled between them in the thick air. "Ethan…"

He winced. "So you have met another man?"

She slowly turned back to face him. Her hazel eyes glimmered with emotions. An apology? Regrets? Indecision? "Yes."

A frown thinned his lips as he reached out and twisted a loose strand of her hair between his fingers. "Who is he, Bec?"

"Ethan, it's not important—"

"Who is he?" He hadn't meant to sound so demanding, but his voice came out cold. Harsh.

She closed her eyes for a brief second, then blinked and met his gaze again. This time conviction and determination darkened the hues. "A stockbroker."

His jaw tightened. "That's the reason you're doing this, so you can be free and clear to be with him."

The silence that stretched between them hammered home his fears.

"I'm sorry, Ethan. But yes. I'm…lonely." She hesitated. "I'm sure you've been with other women."

She'd be shocked to know that he hadn't. He hadn't had the desire. Because no one could ever replace Rebecca.

He couldn't help himself. He slid his hand up her neck, caught the back of her head with his palm and leaned toward her. Her mouth was only inches away. He desperately wanted to kiss her. Feel her pulse throb beneath his touch. Make her forget wanting any man except him. "You don't have to be lonely, Bec."

Her eyes misted. "That's not fair, Ethan. You know I care about you. I always will. You're Jesse's father—"

"Is that all I am to you now?"

She licked her lips, drawing his attention to the curve of her mouth. The one he wanted to taste again. "No, of course not. We share a past. We…loved each other once."

Once? The word triggered a spasm of pain in his chest. She didn't love him anymore….

"But our marriage wasn't working, Ethan, and you know it." Her voice grew stronger.

"I never meant to hurt you, and I know you didn't want to hurt me. It... Our lives just got in the way."

"And your life won't get in the way with this stockbroker?"

"I don't know," she said. "But it's time to try."

He heard the honesty in her answer, and a pang of guilt assaulted him. He wanted her to be happy. "I never meant to neglect you," he said softly.

"I know." She pressed a hand to his cheek. "But we have to think of Jesse. Closure will be good for all of us."

His throat thickened. How could a broken family be good for their son?

Despair thickened his throat. He'd vowed to be a better father than his old man, a better husband. But he'd failed at both. "I am thinking of Jesse. He's my son, Rebecca. He deserves two parents."

"You'll always be his father, Ethan. You can see him whenever you want. That isn't going to change."

Did she really believe that another man in the picture wouldn't alter things?

"Let's face the truth," she said. "You're three thousand miles away. Jesse needs a stable male role model."

He heard her unspoken words. *One who was in his life on a daily basis.* God, he was being selfish, wasn't he? "This man…Jesse likes him?"

She nodded. "He seems to care about Jesse, too."

Her words both soothed him and tore him up inside. Another man was on the verge of replacing him, both in her life and in his son's, and he couldn't stop it from happening.

"We can't rehash the past," she said in a voice filled with emotions. "I want you to be happy, Ethan. You are who you are. I realized long ago I had no right to change that, and I wouldn't want to."

And he had no right to hold her back if this man was what she wanted. Not when he hadn't changed. He still worked ninety hours a week. Still accepted dangerous Eclipse missions. Still thrived on work.

Hell, he lived for the high and the danger. He didn't know how to live *without* it.

Rebecca deserved better.

He dropped his hand, let it rest by his side for a minute, hoping to calm his shaking fingers.

Then he gathered his courage and reached for the pen to sign the papers.

REBECCA HATED SECOND-GUESSING herself. She hated even more the pain in Ethan's eyes when she'd admitted her interest in another man. Guilt and affection for Ethan warred with the need to end the meeting as quickly as possible.

She shouldn't feel guilty. How often had she seen Ethan the past two years? Even Jesse had been disappointed time and time again when Ethan had been forced to cancel.

Frank Sullivan was a nice man. A stock-broker who made good money. A man who had expressed interest in Jesse and coached the kid's baseball team when he had no children of his own. He supported her career and lived close by, so that he could provide more of a stable influence on Jesse. After all, Jesse was growing up. He needed a man in his life. One he could count on.

One who didn't disappear for weeks at a

time, put his life on the line constantly. One who came home at night.

"Bec?"

She spread her hands in her lap. "What is it, Ethan?"

"Can I see Jesse later?"

Her heart twisted, and she clutched Ethan's hand. "Of course you can. Jesse is your son. He loves you."

A muscle ticked in his jaw. "I don't intend to let him forget me."

"I know that," Rebecca said softly. "And I would never let that happen, either." She squeezed his arm. God, this was harder than she'd imagined. "No one can ever replace you in his life, Ethan." *Or in my heart.*

But she had to give Frank Sullivan a chance.

"Thank you for saying that." He rubbed her hand gently. He used to do that, then he'd lift her fingers and kiss them. Then she would melt in his arms.

She couldn't let it go that far today, or she'd never be able to sign these divorce papers. And even if they did kiss or make love, their lifestyles wouldn't change.

"It wasn't all bad, was it?" he asked quietly.

She smiled and shook her head. "No, Ethan. We had some wonderful times, some great memories. But reliving them…it's just too painful."

"The last thing I want is to hurt you," Ethan said quietly.

Her gaze met his. "I know that, Ethan."

"Right." He released her hand and scrubbed his through his short military-cut hair. "Well, then, why procrastinate any longer?"

He handed her the pen and gestured for her to go first. Her insides trembled, but she sat down and zeroed in on the lines where they were supposed to sign their names. How ironic, she thought. After so much love and time together, so many memories and promises, all they had to do to dissolve their marriage and erase the past was scribble their signatures on the dotted line.

She inhaled a deep breath, and pressed the tip of the pen down, when the door suddenly burst open.

"Miss Rebecca! Miss Rebecca!" Jesse's

nanny stumbled into the salon, waving her arms, looking harried.

Rebecca frowned. "What is it, DeeDee?"

"Miss Rebecca," DeeDee sobbed. "Oh, my God, my God, my God. It's Jesse!"

Rebecca shot to her feet, her heart pounding as she searched behind the woman for her son. "Where is he, DeeDee? What's happened?"

Ethan lurched toward DeeDee, grabbed her by the arms and shook her gently. "What's wrong? Is Jesse hurt? Did he have an accident?"

DeeDee's face crumpled and tears streaked her pale cheeks. "No, he's…missing," she sobbed. "I turned my back for just a minute, and he was gone!"

Missing…gone… The room spun.

"Where were you?" Ethan barked.

"At Frog Pond," DeeDee cried. "Miss Rebecca, she told me to take Jesse wading, and so I did. He was so excited. And there were other kids there, so many. They were laughing and playing chase at the edge of the water and he joined in." She heaved a breath. "Then suddenly he disappeared. I searched everywhere, I yelled for him, but he was nowhere! Miss Rebecca, I'm so sorry…"

Rebecca swayed and reached for something to hold on to. Jesse was missing. "No…"

Black dots danced before her eyes just before the world went dark. She felt herself spiraling, floating, the shock clawing at her as she collapsed against Ethan.

ETHAN CAUGHT REBECCA, HIS OWN heart pounding with fear. His son, his five-year-old little boy, was missing. Had he wandered through the crowd and gotten lost, or had he been kidnapped?

He helped Rebecca to a sofa and settled her onto the cushions. "Rebecca?"

"Ethan—"

"Hang on, sweetheart. I'm here."

A gut-wrenching cry rose from deep in her throat. "Jesse?"

"We'll find him, I promise." Even as he muttered the assurance, a dozen terrifying scenarios raced through his mind. Jesse being kidnapped by an ax murderer. Or a pedophile. Christ, no, please no…

His knees buckled and he fought for a breath. He couldn't think like that. He couldn't let Rebecca jump onto that horrifying, runaway train of thought, either.

Time was of the essence. If Jesse had been abducted, he was getting farther and farther away by the minute. He had to call the police.

He reached for his cell phone, then halted. He'd seen enough cases to know that kidnappers always warned against calling the cops. They usually wanted money.

Money—he had lots of it. That was the reason they'd taken Jesse.

He'd give them whatever they asked for, just as long as they didn't hurt his son.

He turned to DeeDee, who had slumped into the nearest wingback chair, crying into her hands.

He had to stop thinking like a father and think like a detective. But Jesse was his son. How could he not think like a father? "DeeDee, did you call for help at the pond?"

She nodded. "I told people all around me and they looked, too. Then this lady said she thought she saw Jesse walking away with a man."

He punched in the number for his Eclipse contact, Dana Whitley, the only civilian who knew about its existence. A secretary for the Pentagon by day, she clandestinely coordinated Eclipse and could accomplish anything.

Ethan explained the situation. "My son has been kidnapped. I need people now to search the area surrounding Frog Pond. This has to be discreet. I don't want it to look like I've called the cops. The kidnapper might be watching."

Rebecca shuddered next to him, and he hung up and squeezed her hands. "Bec, listen, we have to go back to my place. If a kidnapper took him and wants a ransom, he might call me there."

"What about the police?"

"Let's go to my place first. If there's no call or note, then we'll phone it in."

Rebecca latched on to his hand and dragged herself to a sitting position. "But, Ethan, they can search the streets, the highways. Issue an Amber alert—"

Ethan glanced at his phone in a panic and

willed the infuriating thing to ring. He wanted that call, dammit. Wanted to know who had his son and why. "Trust me. My team is on it. They'll cover the streets better than the cops. We have connections, Bec."

He flipped on the handset and noticed a text message waiting. He'd been so busy last night during the blackout he'd finally shut down his phone and ignored any messages.

He checked it now.

"Are you afraid of the dark?"

His blood ran cold. The cryptic message struck a nerve. It had something to do with Jesse's kidnapper. He knew it in his gut.

Fear choked him.

If he hadn't ignored the message last night, maybe he could have prevented his son from being abducted.

FINN SMILED TO HIMSELF AS HE drove the dark sedan into the abandoned warehouse. He would have loved to have been a fly on the wall when Ethan Matalon discovered his precious son was missing. And Rebecca...he would have enjoyed being beside her to offer her comfort. Dry her tears. Whisper reassurances.

Maybe even strip her and soothe her with a night of lovemaking.

His sex swelled, reminding him that he had done without that pleasure for too long. Hell, he'd wanted Rebecca but had forced himself not to push her for fear of raising suspicion. But in the end, maybe he'd screw her anyway.

For now, though, contact with her was too dangerous. Better for her to think he was completely out of the country, off on business.

They would figure out the connection soon enough.

Then Rebecca would blame herself.

As Ethan was no doubt doing, thanks to the text message.

Finn killed the engine, climbed out and shut the warehouse door, then stared at the backseat, where he'd stuffed the boy. The cough syrup in his soda had worked perfectly. The kid was out cold.

But he would wake soon. And like a lot of other children, Jesse Matalon was afraid of the dark.

Ethan had been, too, as a kid. Liam had noted that in his file.

He'd also said that Ethan was smart. He'd know better than to call the cops.

And if he got stupid and called them anyway, then his son's death would be on *his* conscience, not Finn's.

Chapter Three

Shock immobilized Rebecca. This couldn't be happening. Not to her precious little boy. She'd just seen him an hour ago. He'd been smiling and waving his wand, excited about wading in the pond.

And now some stranger had stolen him.

Who would have done such a thing?

Her mind blurred with the gruesome possibilities. Only monsters preyed on small children. Sick, twisted, perverted creatures who took advantage of their innocence. Ones who tortured and hurt and murdered.

"Stop thinking," Ethan commanded. He squeezed her arm gently. "Look at me, Rebecca. I know you're terrified, and you're imagining the worst, but stop it. We have to pull ourselves together."

"But, Ethan—" Her voice broke on a sob.

"I know, baby. I know." He dragged her into his arms and held her, rocking her back and forth. She felt the fine tremors in his big body and knew he was struggling with his own terror.

"I swear, Bec, I'll get Jesse back. And I'll kill the monster who kidnapped him."

She gripped his arms and heaved, suddenly nauseated. "What if it's too late, Ethan? What if—"

"Shh. Don't go there. We have to stay positive." He pressed his finger to her lips, his dark brown eyes glinting with rage and other emotions. Fear. Panic. Determination.

Love for his son.

"I have money," he said. "Whoever has Jesse will want it. I'll pay them however much they want. But now we need to go back to my place. They may call there."

"I don't understand why Jesse would go with some man," Rebecca said. "We've talked about strangers. He should have yelled for help."

"I don't understand, either," Ethan said. "Maybe he tricked him somehow."

"What about my hotel?" Rebecca asked. "What if the man who has him calls *me?* I'm a television personality. Maybe someone wants to hurt me."

"We'll look into that angle," Ethan conceded.

DeeDee cleared her throat and dropped to her knees in front of Rebecca, her eyes red-rimmed and swollen. "I'll wait in the hotel room for the call. I won't leave the phone for a second. I swear. I'll do everything I can to help get Jesse back safely."

Ethan glanced at Rebecca with questions in his eyes. For a brief second, Rebecca's chest tightened with another thought. What if DeeDee had something to do with the kidnapping?

She had checked the girl out before she had hired her. She'd had an impeccable reputation, excellent references and had worked as a nanny for two years for another family until they'd moved abroad. Ethan had also used his connections with Eclipse to make certain she was trustworthy. DeeDee was even studying early childhood education and wanted to be a kindergarten teacher.

Still, Rebecca had to ask. She wiped at the tears blurring her eyes. "DeeDee, how do we know that you didn't have something to do with Jesse's disappearance? Maybe you need money for school or…or something else."

DeeDee jerked back as if Rebecca had slapped her. "Miss Rebecca, you can't think that. I love Jesse." She hugged her arms around her waist as if to hold herself together. "I would never do anything to hurt or endanger Jesse. I swear. He's like my own little brother."

Ethan gave her a concerned look. But they'd be foolish not to question DeeDee. "Rebecca…there was a text message on my phone from last night. I think it may have something to do with the kidnapping."

"What did it say?"

He showed it to her and she gasped. "My heavens, Ethan. Whoever took him knows that he's afraid of the dark."

"And that I was when I was a kid," Ethan said.

She gripped his hand. Ethan had been

trapped in a storm drain when he was four. He had had nightmares for years about the incident.

"We need to hurry. I want to check the house." He gestured toward DeeDee. "Wait in the hotel room, and let us know if anyone calls."

She nodded, pushing to her feet. "I promise I'll do whatever you tell me."

"You'd better," Ethan said harshly. "Because if I find out that you conspired in the kidnapping of our son, then I'll make sure you pay." His eyes darkened. "And trust me, Miss Archer, you won't like the punishment."

ETHAN FORCED HIMSELF INTO combat mode. His military training and work with Eclipse had taught him how to channel emotions, to compartmentalize and focus.

Damn lot of good it was doing him.

He kept seeing his little boy's innocent, terrified face in his mind, and panic shot through him. What was Jesse thinking? Was he okay? What had the sick person who'd taken him done to him?

Stop it, he ordered himself. He'd told

Rebecca they had to think positively, and he had to heed his own advice. If he fell apart, she definitely would.

He had to take charge and get their son back. He couldn't let anything happen to Jesse.

"Let's check your room first." He helped Rebecca to stand, and she seemed to summon her courage and led the way to the stairwell. The three of them climbed the five floors, sweating, the tension thickening as Rebecca removed her key and let them into the plush room. Ethan glanced quickly around but saw nothing amiss. Rebecca had chosen a suite for her and Jesse with an adjoining room for the nanny. She checked the hotel phone for messages and found none.

Of course, the power had been out. He surveyed the room, his heart tugging painfully at the sight of Jesse's toy cars and the walkie-talkie set he'd given him for his last birthday. He wished Jesse had it with him now.

To cover the bases, he insisted on checking DeeDee's room. She immediately acceded, and within minutes, he confirmed that the room was clean.

Still, he'd phone his contact at Eclipse and put someone on her. They'd follow her every move, check her phone records, her computer, e-mails, just in case...

"Stay here and don't leave for any reason," Ethan told DeeDee. "I'll send over a bodyguard."

"A bodyguard?" DeeDee looked even more shaken.

He nodded. It was as much for his peace of mind, to have someone watch her, as it was for her protection, but he didn't tell her. If the kidnapper had wanted her, he would have forced her to go with him, too.

The minute hand on the wall clock turned. It seemed like hours since DeeDee had made the announcement about Jesse being missing, but in fact, it had only been minutes. Precious minutes, though, that counted.

Ethan raced down the steps, pulling Rebecca along behind him. Outside, he scanned the streets for any signs of his son as they climbed in his car and slowly made their way through the traffic to his brownstone.

Rebecca was pale, her eyes glassy, her

body rigid with shock. He pulled into his driveway and parked, took her hand and they jumped out, then hurried up the sidewalk. The sight of a note tucked beneath the brass doorknocker made him halt.

"Ethan?"

He yanked the note free and opened the folded piece of paper. His heart slammed against his ribs as he read the message he'd feared.

I have Jesse. You'll never see him again if you call the cops.

"OH, NO. ETHAN..." Rebecca had tried to hold on to the hope that Jesse had simply wandered off in the crowd. That a Good Samaritan had found him by now and that they had called the police. Or that Jesse had told them where he was staying and that he was on his way back to the Ritz.

But the note confirmed her worst fears.

Ethan made a low sound of pain and frustration, then curved his arm around her and pulled her up against him. "Bec..."

His strangled voice sent another shiver of terror down her spine.

Then he spun around as if scanning the area to see if the person who'd left the note was nearby. The realization hit Rebecca, too. The kidnapper or a conspirator might be watching to make sure they found the message. To see if they phoned the police.

She blinked back tears and studied the passers-by. Due to the blackout, the streets looked grim. People walked in a hurry, shaken and wary of others. Cars still clogged the street, creating a nightmare for drivers. And two uniformed officers tried to direct the mob and clean up the congestion at the intersections. Another one walked the streets as if to announce his presence in case burglars or vandals decided to take advantage of nonfunctioning security systems in the moneyed Beacon Hill section.

But she saw no one who stuck out as watching them. No one with a scared little boy in tow.

"There's no ransom," Ethan mumbled. "I don't understand why there's no ransom."

"There will be," she said, battling terror at the distress in his voice. "They're going to call, Ethan. They have to."

He gave a clipped nod, removed his keys and unlocked the door. They rushed inside, and he hurried to check his machine, then cursed. Of course, the blasted thing wasn't working because of the blackout.

"Let me check the brownstone. Stay put, Rebecca."

Shaking, she sank onto the living room couch, and twisted her fingers together while he searched the rooms on all three stories. Last night she'd assured Jesse there were no monsters. But today, in broad daylight, one had stolen him.

Ethan returned, shaking his head, but he was already on his cell phone. On the coffee table, she spotted the photo of Ethan with their son at a baseball game, picked it up and traced her finger over Jesse's smiling face. Disbelief warred with hopelessness, but she fought through it, grappled for strength.

Their baby had to be all right.

She couldn't survive losing her son.

ETHAN PRAYED SILENTLY AS HE phoned Eclipse teammate Ty Jones, whose day job was as a Secret Service agent. The note had said no cops, and Ethan would comply. But he needed help, and his cohorts from the Eclipse team were the best. He didn't intend to sit idly by while some maniac stole his son and got away with it.

Fear niggled at the base of his spine. Why hadn't there been a ransom note or a call yet?

What did the kidnapper want if not money?

Ty sounded winded when he answered the call. "Ethan, I've been trying to reach you. Dana phoned me and told me about your son."

"There was a note warning me not to call the cops," Ethan said gruffly. "But no ransom. Ty, I don't understand."

"Sit tight. I'll be there in five minutes."

Ethan hung up and moved to the window to study the street, searching the crowd and shadowy corners. He didn't expect to see Jesse outside, but maybe he'd get a glimpse of someone watching the house. Someone he would chase down and beat into telling him where he had his little boy.

His fingers ached from gripping the cell phone in his hands. He willed it to ring, to be the kidnapper with a message relaying his demands. Where to make the drop.

How to get his son back.

His chest tightened painfully. He had to be strong for Rebecca. For Jesse. Had to hold it together until he found the bastard who'd done this.

Fury raged through his veins like fire ripping through dry kindling. Then he'd kill the maniac with his bare hands, making sure he suffered before he died.

A pounding on the front door jarred him back to motion. He rushed to let Ty in. His friend looked disheveled, rough around the edges as if he hadn't slept all night.

Ty said hello to Rebecca, then leaned against the fireplace wall with his hands fisted by his sides. "I think I know who kidnapped your son."

The air froze in Ethan's lungs. Rebecca

started to stand, but Ty gestured for her to remain seated.

"Who?" Ethan asked. "What's going on, Ty?"

"I tried to reach you earlier, Ethan. To warn you."

"What the hell are you talking about?" Ethan's patience snapped like a thin wire beneath too much pressure. "I want to know who has Jesse, and I want to know now."

Ty sighed. "I believe Liam Shea is behind Jesse's disappearance."

"Liam?" The name caused a cold ball of dread in Ethan's stomach. "What? Why?"

"Who is Liam Shea?" Rebecca asked.

Ethan scrubbed a hand through his hair. "Ten years ago, a group of us formed a select coterie of Special Forces servicemen in a high-profile rescue mission. Fifty-eight people had been taken hostage in a civil war-torn Middle Eastern nation, most of them American, including the Secretary of State, Geoffrey Rollins." Ethan paused. "Commander Tom Bradley recruited seven of us to get them out alive. Liam Shea was the electrical expert, Shane Peters the security expert, engine man Chase Vickers, me and Ty, the demolitions man. Vice-President Grant Davis was the tactical specialist then, and Frederic LeBron, a prince from Beau Pays, was the language expert."

"I don't understand what any of this has to do with Jesse," Rebecca cried.

Ethan sat down beside her and took her hands in his. "It's a long story, Bec. Suffice to say the mission went awry. The timing was off, and the mission blew up in our faces. Cyanide gas was released. By some miracle, we lost only three hostages. Liam was wounded but Grant saved his life. When all was said and done, Grant was hailed a hero."

"And Liam?" Rebecca asked.

"He was court-martialed, dishonorably discharged and has spent the past ten years in prison."

"He's out of jail now," Ty cut in. "And he wants revenge."

Rebecca gasped and dropped her head into her hands, breathing deeply as if she might pass out. Ethan stroked her back, although his own chest ached and his pulse raced with fear.

"The blackout," Ty said. "We think Liam is responsible."

"For the entire blackout?" Rebecca asked.

Ty nodded. "Liam has blown up two BP and L power plants in town." He turned to Ethan. "He's just beginning. Last night LeBron's daughter, Princess Ariana, was in town for the celebration of an international trade agreement. She joined dignitaries from around the world at the John Hancock Tower. President Stack and the vice-president were there, too."

Ethan's stomach turned to lead. "Ty works as Secret Service for the vice-president," he explained to Rebecca.

"I still don't see what this has to do with Jesse," she whispered.

"It's part of Liam's master plan of revenge," Ty said. He angled his head toward Ethan. "Shane was there last night, too. He planned to test the security surrounding the Beau Pays sapphire on exhibition from Prince Frederick. The party was in full swing when the blackout occurred. It was a freaking nightmare for all of the Secret Service and guests." Ty made a disgusted sound. "Shane received a message about that time. It said, 'Are you afraid of the dark'?"

Ethan gripped his phone with shaking hands. "I received the same message."

Ty didn't seem surprised. He continued, "As soon as the lights went out, goggled men swarmed the building and took everyone hostage. They threatened to kill the attendees if the president and vice-president didn't show themselves."

"What happened?" Ethan asked.

"Stack and Grant handed themselves over. The men tried to leave with them, but in the confusion, the president escaped. He's fine now, but Grant is still missing."

"This crazy man has the vice-president?" Rebecca asked in horror.

"We think so," Ty confirmed.

"Liam targeted Grant for revenge," Ethan said, the full picture forming in his mind.

Ty nodded again. "The entire Special Forces team is being targeted, Ethan. Shane and Chase have already been hit."

Ethan dreaded the answer to his next question. "Are they all right?"

"Shane survived. But not before having to deal with Colin Shea, one of Liam's sons."

"His sons are involved?" Ethan asked.

"Up to their eyeballs." Ty shifted.

"Liam's sons were close to their father," Ethan continued, "and blamed the Eclipse team for his arrest. They think we betrayed Liam."

Ty sighed. "Colin wanted the sapphire. Shane tried to protect the stone, as well as Princess Ariana. Thankfully, Ben Parker, one of the FBI agents Shane has worked with in the past, managed to divert the shooter and Shane escaped."

"Thank God," Ethan said. "What about Chase?"

"Liam's other son, Aidan Shea, climbed into Chase's limo, pretending to be a dignitary. He pulled a gun, threatened Chase, then escaped."

Ethan propped his elbows on his knees and leaned into his hands. "Is Chase all right?"

"Yes. But Aidan claimed he'd lose everything that mattered to him."

Ethan contemplated the threat. For him, it meant Jesse. For Chase? "Lily?"

"I'm afraid so. Chase managed to get to the hospital before Aidan got to her." Ty grunted. "She was pregnant."

"Hell, don't tell me Aidan killed her."

"No, they went on the run. Finally Chase called Ben Parker for help. Unfortunately Parker was killed. Chase called me to warn me about what was going on, that Liam Shea was involved, and that he suspected Liam had something even bigger planned."

"And now Jesse is missing." Ethan released a string of expletives.

Rebecca's soft cry twisted his heart. "He took our son to get back at you?"

Guilt slammed into Ethan. Rebecca was right. It was his fault their son was missing. That mission ten years ago had brought this horror on them now.

He remembered Liam's fury at the court-martial hearing. The rage in his eyes when he'd been sentenced to prison. His vow of revenge.

Liam didn't care whom he hurt, as long

as he paid them back for what he saw as their betrayal.

And poor little Jesse was being used as a pawn in his twisted plan.

Ethan shook with the force of his fear. He knew Liam well, had witnessed how irate and focused he could be.

God help them.

He didn't want to tell Rebecca, but Liam was cold-hearted enough to kill Jesse to get back at him.

Chapter Four

Rebecca lowered her head into her hands and inhaled a deep breath, trying to calm her raging emotions. Yet her head spun with the implications of Ty's comments.

One look into Ethan's face, and the turmoil and guilt in his eyes robbed her breath. She had never seen her strong, tough husband look so terrified. That alone magnified the fear mounting in her chest.

His work for the military had been important and top secret. Though he'd never spoken of it, she'd known it had been dangerous.

But she'd never contemplated the fact that her son's life might be in jeopardy because of what Ethan had done.

Ty's explanation for the blackout confirmed how twisted and desperate this man Liam was. And his sons…they must have been planning their revenge for years. They'd undoubtedly covered their tracks, knew what they were doing, how to orchestrate their plan without being detected.

Which one of them had taken Jesse? What were they doing to him now? They could be anywhere in Boston—the seaport district, Cambridge, the North End, Chinatown—or he could have hopped a plane and taken him someplace far away.

Was he alive or had they killed him?

No, don't think like that. He has to be all right.

Memories of Jesse's smiling face at the ballgame yesterday flitted through her mind. He'd been so disappointed that Ethan hadn't shown, but as soon as the game had started, he'd gotten swept up in the excitement, and he'd yelled and pounded his small hand into his glove, hoping to catch a foul ball. Later, she'd laughed as he'd crammed a hot dog into his mouth, and ketchup and mustard had dribbled down his chin.

And when the game had ended, he'd jumped up and down, shouting that he wished his dad could have been there to see the win.

She'd been so angry at Ethan…

Now Jesse might never have the chance to see another game or his father again.

She closed her eyes and summoned her courage. She remembered the way he'd tucked his small hand inside hers as they'd woven through the crowded stadium on the way out. The gleam in his smile when he'd spotted one of the players signing autographs.

He'd trusted her to take care of him, but she had failed. Now he was all alone….

A strangled sound clogged her throat, and she jumped up and ran to the bathroom. Inside, she splashed cold water on her face, trembling violently. She didn't want to blame Ethan, yet his past had brought this horror on their innocent little boy.

She leaned against the sink, again seeing Jesse's trusting small face in her mind, and a sob escaped her. After the first memory came, others followed, and she sagged onto the floor in a heap, raised her knees, propped her arms on them and let the tears fall.

A second later, the door squeaked open, and Ethan sank down beside her, took her in his arms and held her.

"I'm sorry," she whispered, hating herself for falling apart. She needed to be strong, yet she couldn't control the flood of emotions.

"Shh, he's our baby," Ethan said gruffly. "You wouldn't be a mother if you weren't upset."

She gulped back tears and leaned into him, savoring his strength and comforting arms. He rocked her, soothing her with gentle strokes and whispered promises that he would find Jesse and bring him safely home.

But his words only triggered her anger. He'd muttered false promises before. Hadn't he sworn he'd be there when Jesse was born? Instead he'd been away on business and she'd almost delivered their baby all alone. The other times he'd disappointed her and Jesse came crashing back, making the pressure in her chest unbearable, and she pulled away.

"You've made promises before, Ethan.

How can I trust you now?" The need to blame someone, to vent, surged through her. "This is all your fault. You and your job. It was always more important than us. And now our son's life is on the line because of it."

Ethan's face hardened and he balled his hands into fists. "I promise you, Bec. I may have let you both down before, but this time I won't. I swear it."

Pain thickened his voice, but Rebecca saw other images in her mind. The disappointment in Jesse's eyes the night Ethan hadn't come home to help them decorate the Christmas tree. His silent tears another time when Ethan had missed Jesse's first Little League game. The crude family sketch Jesse had drawn this year in kindergarten, a picture of the three of them and a new baby, the little brother Jesse had asked Santa for last year.

A baby they would never have, living on opposite sides of the country and divorced.

"I know you mean that, Ethan. But what if we—what if *you*—can't save him? What if it's too late already?"

He flinched. "Don't talk like that, Bec. Besides…"

"Besides what, Ethan?" she asked coldly.

"Jesse is more useful alive."

"More useful?" Shock stirred her temper. "What's wrong with you, Ethan? You're talking about Jesse like he's some object, not your own son."

"I didn't mean it like that, Bec, and you know it. I'm trying to think like a cop."

"All I know is that you let us walk out of your life once before. You were ready to sign the divorce papers, so I assume you want me out of your life."

He didn't move, simply met her look with a dark, piercing gaze that sliced through her, reopening painful wounds.

"You're the one who wanted the papers signed so you could get on with your life," he said bitterly.

Only because he hadn't wanted them enough to try.

She ached for him to hold her now, yearned to believe that he could make this right, but she couldn't allow herself to believe in him again, to trust him. She and Jesse had been hurt too many times before.

So she wrapped her anger around her instead. She'd come here to end their marriage. And she would—once they found Jesse.

ETHAN SPUN AWAY FROM REBECCA, his chest aching. She was right to blame him. The situation was all his fault. He was responsible for the agony in Rebecca's cries, the fear in her eyes. And the fact that his son was in the hands of a madman.

"I know you hate me, Rebecca, but I love our son and I'll do everything in my power to bring him back."

"I don't hate you, Ethan," she said, although her look condemned him in his soul. "But I can't trust you, either. When this is over, it might be best for you to stay away from Jesse."

Her soft voice twisted the knife of guilt piercing his chest. But she was right.

He was a failure as a father and husband. As much as he'd loved her, he hadn't been able to give himself wholly.

And Jesse deserved to be safe. He didn't deserve to be in the hands of Liam Shea, to be a ploy in his revenge plot.

The cold wave of terror settling inside him hardened his jaw. But could he really let them both go forever when he got Jesse back?

Rage sparked his temper, pushing the guilt and heartache into the back of his mind. He had hoped to talk to Rebecca today, let her know that he was going to cut back on his hours, spend more time with his son. His software company had attained the level of success he'd hoped for; he could delegate work and be with Jesse. But now he might never get that chance. And Rebecca didn't want him in their lives at all.

"Ethan, do you have a plan? Some way to contact Shea?"

He pivoted, resorted to what he did best.

He might not be a good father, but he was damn good at tracking down terrorists and bad guys. And when it came time to kill, Ethan would have no problem taking out Liam or his sons.

"No, but I will."

Ty poked his head in with a frown. "I need to go, Ethan."

"What do we do now?" Rebecca asked.

A computer ace, Ethan knew how to dig up information.

"Let me see what I can find out about Liam and his sons." Grateful he still had some battery left in his computer, Ethan booted up his laptop and typed in several commands, searching the databases Eclipse had access to.

"What are you looking for?" Rebecca asked.

"Everything I can find on them." Ethan scrubbed a hand over his neck. "Where Liam and his sons have been the past few years. Jobs. Addresses. Friends or associates. Anything that might give us a clue where they're hiding out, or where they've taken Jesse."

A photo of Liam appeared on the screen. Ethan frowned, his mind sweeping him back ten years to that fateful mission.

The hostages, mostly engineers, teachers and missionaries, were being held in a densely populated downtown, in the cavern-like basement of a closely guarded building. The world had prayed for their release for weeks. Every country from which the hostages had hailed—the U.S., England, Australia and the Alpine nation Beau Pays—had attempted a rescue and failed.

Ethan's Special Forces team had been the last hope.

The men had methodically outlined their plan. Just as Ty ignited a minor explosion as a diversion, Liam was to kill the power to the building, plunging it into darkness to provide cover for the team's entrance. The eight of them, armed with high-tech surveillance to see where the hostages were being held, were in place to take out the guards in precision timing down to the nanosecond.

Previous rescuers had reported that the captors had scrambled all frequencies in the building, allowing no communication between team members. Commander Bradley was supposed to give a visual cue.

But something had gone wrong.

Sweat rolled down Ethan's neck as he remembered the events. Shea, claiming he'd seen Bradley's signal, had killed the lights prematurely, causing the captors to release cyanide gas. Among the chaos, it was a miracle anyone had gotten out alive.

"Ethan?"

Rebecca's soft voice jerked him from the traumatic memory. When he glanced up, he saw her watching him warily. "What is it?" she asked.

"Nothing." He turned back to the computer, clicked a few more keys, and photographs of Liam's boys spilled onto the screen.

Which one of them had Jesse? Liam or one of his sons?

He forced a chokehold on his emotions and began to think not like a computer wiz but like an Eclipse team member. If the Sheas had been planning this attack for a while, they had no doubt been watching each one of their targets. Liam wouldn't implement his plan without extensive research. He'd know everything about each of them, their daily routines, where they shopped, whom they talked to on the damn phone. He'd probably had them under surveillance for months.

They'd been watching Rebecca.

The notion chilled him. But he knew he

was right. Hadn't Ty told him they knew about Lily Garrett, Chase Vickers's only love? Shea would cover all his bases, including Rebecca.

A cold anger settled into his bones. One of them had stalked her, pried into her life, probably watched her at work, in her house, in her kitchen, her bedroom...

He cleared his throat to swallow back the bile. He had to find Jesse first. Then it would be payback time for Liam and his sons. And if one of them harmed Jesse or Rebecca, he'd find out what torture could be like.

"Rebecca, come here," he said. "If Liam or one of his sons has Jesse, they would have been watching you, waiting on the right time to grab Jesse. Look at these photos and tell me if you recognize anyone."

His heart hammered as she stepped closer and sat down beside him to study the screen.

A SHIVER TORE THROUGH Rebecca at the thought that one of these men might have been stalking her, shadowing her and Jesse's every move.

Shaking with the realization of having her privacy violated, she stared at Liam Shea's face, memorizing every inch. Her stomach clenched at the icy coldness in his eyes. He was a formidable man, one with no heart. A man who had obviously suffered; who'd had ten years to let his anger fester and to plot his revenge—one who was so full of hate he wouldn't care if he hurt her child.

Emotions threatened to choke her, but she tamped them back as two other men's faces appeared on screen.

"The one on the left is Colin Shea," Ty pointed out. "And that's Aidan. After Liam was arrested, his wife, Margaret, divorced him and moved her sons out of Massachusetts. She couldn't stand the publicity and shame. After that, they moved around the Pacific Northwest for a while and eventually settled into Lawrenceville, a small town in Oregon."

"Margaret thought her husband was guilty?" Rebecca asked.

Ty nodded. "Colin and Aidan later moved to the Cascade Mountains in Washington State and bought a cabin. They opened a business selling and renting outdoor recreational equipment. That business gave them the anonymity they wanted."

"Colin had planned a military career," Ethan said. "But after his father was court-martialed, he abandoned that aspiration and moved out west. He and Aidan totally devoted themselves to Liam."

"How do you know all this?" Rebecca asked.

Ty and Ethan exchanged furtive looks. "The team has kept an eye on them ever since Liam's arrest."

"You expected retaliation?" Rebecca said on a shaky breath.

Ethan shrugged. "You don't work Special Forces without learning to be cautious."

"And suspicious," Ty added.

Ethan grunted. "At Liam's court-martial hearing, he made it pretty plain that he blamed the team."

"You should have told me, Ethan, warned me," Rebecca said, anger hardening her voice. "If I'd known, I would have done more to protect Jesse. I would have alerted the nanny, never left Jesse with her."

A muscle ticked in Ethan's jaw, but he didn't defend himself or deny the fact that she had a right to her bitter accusations.

Ty pointed to the screen. "Colin was the one who came after the gem last night. It was Beau Pays and Frederick's most prized possession, and he thought losing it would ruin the royal family's name the way his father had been ruined."

"They're hitting each of us at our most vulnerable spot," Ethan surmised.

For a brief second, pain engulfed Rebecca. She wanted to press a hand to Ethan's shoulder, comfort him and take back her words, but she couldn't make herself move. Ethan should have told her about the Sheas.

"Do you recognize Colin or Liam, Rebecca?"

"No."

"How about Colin's brother?" Ethan said. "Study Aidan."

"Aidan assisted in kidnapping Grant Davis," Ty continued, "but he escaped and hijacked Chase."

Panic threatened Rebecca again as she

realized the extent of these men's plans. "He doesn't look familiar, either."

Ethan scrolled down and another picture appeared. This man appeared to be in his late twenties, with green eyes, a wide-set jaw, a thin tapered nose and a high forehead.

Something about his face struck a chord of recognition within Rebecca.

"This is Finn, the middle son," Ethan said.

"That's Finn Shea?" Rebecca narrowed her eyes, analyzing the photo in more detail.

"Yes," Ty said. "He was always pushing the envelope, a troublemaker. But he's just as loyal to his father as the other brothers. Do you recognize him?"

"I'm not sure." Something about the man in the photo was familiar. She couldn't shake the feeling she'd seem him somewhere. At the market? The TV station? On her street? Could he have been with DeeDee at some point?

She leaned closer, the set to his jaw again sparking a seed of familiarity. She pictured him with black hair, shorn short, his jaw more angular, his nose thinner....

Sucking in a sharp breath, she studied his eyes. Change the eye color and— "Oh, God."

Ethan jerked his head toward her. "What is it, Bec? Have you seen him?"

She gripped the desk edge with clammy fingers. "I...think I may know him."

A muscle ticked in Ethan's jaw. "How? Did you see him somewhere? The hotel today?"

She shook her head, her body shuddering. "With a couple changes he could be Frank Sullivan."

"Sullivan?" Ethan mumbled.

Ty cleared his throat. "Sullivan was the last name the Sheas adopted after Liam was court-martialed."

"Oh, Jesus." Rebecca swayed, her entire world slipping off its axis again.

Ethan steadied her with one hand. "How do you know him?"

Her voice caught. "Frank Sullivan is the man I told you about. The one I'm involved with." She jerked away, paced across the room. "But Frank wouldn't hurt Jesse. He cares about him." She paused, met Ethan's gaze and willed her heart to stop pounding.

"He even started coaching Jesse's Little League team to get to know him better."

As soon as she said the words, Rebecca realized the truth.

"So Jesse would have gone with him willingly," Ty said. "Not screamed or shouted about a stranger?"

Ethan simply stared at her with accusations in his eyes. Rebecca clutched her stomach and doubled over as the truth dawned.

She had been such a fool. Frank Sullivan was Finn Shea. He'd disguised himself, then befriended her as part of his grand scheme to kidnap her son.

And she'd fallen right into his devious hands.

Here she had blamed Ethan, but it was her fault Jesse had been kidnapped.

Her fault because she had been lonely and had invited a vengeful potential killer into their lives.

Chapter Five

For the second time in hours, Ethan felt as if he'd been punched in the stomach. To think that Rebecca had been interested in another man cut to the core, but for that man to be Finn Shea, Liam's son, sliced his gut.

The idea of Shea touching her or Jesse made his stomach revolt. His blood boiling with rage, he stood, crossed to the window and stared outside.

"Finn Shea is the man you were divorcing me for?" Ethan asked.

"Yes. I mean no…" Rebecca's strangled sound echoed through the tension-filled room.

Her protest sounded weak, feeble, riddled with guilt. He wanted to go to her and assure her that everything was all right, that he forgave her for getting involved with Finn, but something held him back. Some primitive, possessive jealousy crawled through him like a savage animal and made him want to howl and gnash his teeth. He pictured Finn Shea's hands on her, and bloodlust stirred in his veins. He *would* kill Finn Shea, not only for taking his son but for using his wife. Divorce papers aside, he'd placed a ring on Rebecca's finger and they had exchanged vows. She had given birth to his child. Rebecca was *his* wife.

She always would be in his mind.

"Where is Frank Sullivan now?" he asked between clenched teeth.

"There has to be a mistake," Rebecca said shakily. "Maybe I'm wrong. Maybe this man isn't Frank." Her voice caught. "Frank loved Jesse. He's a stockbroker, he made deals on E-TRADE, he's not a killer. He was into business, not anything dangerous."

How dare she defend the man? "In other words, you thought he was safe?" Ethan whirled around, his hands knotted into fists, barely controlling his rage.

Ty shot him a concerned look, but Ethan ignored him. Ty had no idea what it felt like to have your own child snatched from your hands. To think you might never see him again. To know that one of your enemies had been involved with your wife.

Had she slept with Finn Shea?

"Yes." Her voice wavered. "He was quiet, never spoke harshly to me or Jesse, didn't seem violent at all."

"He pretended to care for him, Rebecca," Ethan ground out. "Face the facts. This man used you to gain access to our son."

And she hadn't suspected a thing.

Anguish darkened her eyes, and she pressed a hand over her mouth, another sob wrenching from her. Guilt exploded in his chest for his harsh tone, but he couldn't bring himself to apologize or comfort her.

He was still trying to erase from his mind the torturous picture of her with Finn Shea. Of Finn Shea doing God knew what to his boy to hurt *him*.

More guilt slammed into Ethan as another realization dawned. If he had been with

Rebecca and Jesse, then Finn—Frank Sullivan—couldn't have seduced her. Then his son would be safe.

"Let's check out the man and see if he is Finn. When did you last see Frank Sullivan?" Ty asked, injecting his calm tone into the volatile emotions vibrating through the room.

Rebecca ran her hands through her hair. He'd seen her do it a thousand times when she was nervous. The gesture was so familiar it started that dull ache in his chest. The one that had nearly immobilized him at times the past two years.

The one that told him he was a fool to have let her go.

"We said goodbye at Logan Airport," she said. "He was going to London on a business trip. Jesse and I dropped him off before the Red Sox game."

Ethan forced himself back to the computer, then ran a check on Frank Sullivan, while Ty phoned the airport to inquire about London flights.

Rebecca dropped into the chair beside Ethan's desk, stone-faced, her fist pressed to her mouth, her body coiled with tension as he researched the man.

Ethan accessed every conceivable database but found nothing on a stockbroker named Frank Sullivan.

"There's no record of a Frank Sullivan or a Finn Shea on a flight from Logan Airport to London," Ty said as he hung up the phone. "In fact, there are no records that he was on any flights out of the city this week."

"According to our databases," Ethan said, "the Frank Sullivan you know, Rebecca, doesn't exist. He's a sham."

"But what about an address in L.A.? His company?" She struggled to recall the firm he worked for and gave Ethan the name.

For the next few minutes, she practically held her breath, praying he'd find something to prove that she was wrong, imagining things. That Frank Sullivan wasn't Finn Shea. That she hadn't been a fool, hadn't endangered Jesse.

She'd let him kiss her, for God's sake.

Ethan hissed beneath his breath, a sound of pure frustration that only heightened her anxiety. "The company name is bogus," he growled. "And I can't find an address for him anywhere." He narrowed his eyes at her. "Do you know where he lived? Did you ever go to his place?"

She hesitated, then shook her head. A small exhale of relief whooshed from his chest.

Ethan hacked into a program the authorities used to check identities, one that could alter appearances with graphics to approximate physical changes a target or criminal might use as a disguise.

"Tell me about his face, Rebecca. The shape, his nose, his jaw."

She did. Then she went on to the other changes. "His hair was short, clipped, military style."

Like Ethan's.

He cut a scathing look her way, and she bit down on her lip as he maneuvered the program. Shea's face.

"And his eyes were blue, not green."

He made the adjustment and Rebecca gasped, all the color draining from her face.

"Oh, God, Ethan, that's him. That's Frank Sullivan." Her voice warbled. "What have I done?"

REBECCA RAN TO THE BATHROOM, slammed the door, then dropped to her knees and purged the contents of her stomach. How could she have been so blind? Her mistake might cost Jesse his life....

Tears dripped down her face, and she reached for a washcloth on the sink, dampened it, then pressed it against her forehead and leaned against the toilet.

It would be night soon. The sky would turn dark, the sun fading in the horizon, the lack of electricity would plunge the city into total blackness.

Jesse would be frightened. Wanting to come home. Wanting to see his father.

She'd promised him he would.

What if she never saw him again? What if...

No, stop it, Rebecca. You're his mother. Jesse is still alive. You'd know it if he wasn't. You'd feel it inside.

Fighting the fear threatening to immobilize

her, she touched her fingers to her mouth, remembering the night she'd first met Frank Sullivan six months ago.

She'd attended a party for a charity event to cover the fund-raiser for a new wing at a nearby children's hospital. Frank had approached her and had initiated conversation. He had seemed charming, sincere, had talked about his donation to the children's wing and how he wished he could do more.

His interest in that hospital and concern for the children had attracted her, although when he'd invited her to dinner the next week, she'd declined his invitation. He had been attractive, but he wasn't Ethan.

Over the past two years, Ethan had become the scale by which she measured every man she met. And no one had made the grade.

That night she'd dragged out the photo album of her and Ethan and had poured over the pictures. She'd almost called Ethan and admitted she wanted to reconcile, that they could piece back together their broken marriage if they tried hard enough.

In fact, she had called, but he'd been away. Then she'd cried herself to sleep.

But the next morning, when she'd awakened to the sun streaming through the window, she'd decided that she wouldn't cry any more over Ethan. It was time for her to stop living in the past and move on.

Frank had called an hour later. She'd thought it was fate.

He had been persistent. He'd asked her to lunch the following week, but she'd still held back. Then he'd volunteered to help coach Jesse's Little League games, and she had finally relented. Seeing him with the young boys, especially her son, who missed his father, had convinced her that Jesse needed a male role model.

She'd thought Frank might be that man.

He'd been so good to Jesse.

Too good to be true.

Anger churned through her. His interest in her and Jesse, his compassion for kids, his coaching, that tender kiss… It had all been an act.

A knock sounded at the door. "Bec?"

Ethan's gruff voice dragged her from the past, back to reality. The horrible reality that had she been smarter and not fallen for Frank Sullivan's devious, charming act, Jesse might be safe now.

He pushed open the door, and she forced herself to stand, blotted her face with the washcloth, then turned to face him.

"Are you all right?"

"No."

Ethan made no move to touch her or console her this time. She didn't deserve to be comforted. Not when she'd acted like a fool.

Once again, they'd reached an impasse and stood miles apart.

It didn't matter. Jesse was the only one who did.

The image of him as a baby, the first time she'd held him, drifted back and she wanted to cry again. She'd promised him she'd take care of him. Better than her mother had cared for her.

But she'd let him down.

"Rebecca, I know you're blaming yourself,"

Ethan said, "we both are, but we have to pull it together if we're going to find Jesse."

She nodded and left the bathroom. She would not give up. She would fight for Jesse until her dying breath. Summoning her strength, she gathered her control and determination. They would find her baby and bring him home. And when she saw Frank Sullivan—Finn Shea—if Ethan didn't kill him, she would.

Ethan followed her to the den. "I need you to think. Did Frank ever mention a place where he might go? A part of the city he preferred, anything about growing up that stood out?"

She shook her head. "He talked about having brothers. Said they were close, that that was the reason he'd decided to help coach the boys."

"What kind of car does he drive?"

"A silver Audi. But his car is in L.A."

"But the Audi tells me he likes expensive cars. Ty, check and see if a Frank Sullivan or Finn Shea rented or purchased a car in the past few days."

Ty nodded and stepped aside to phone Dana and ask for help on that.

"What else?" Ethan asked Rebecca. "How did you meet? Where?"

She related the details of the charity fund-raiser.

She remembered how he'd looked that night. Tall and lean, handsome, charming. He had sky-blue eyes that glittered in the sunlight, not the menacing eyes of a madman seeking revenge.

She paused, anger mounting as she realized the lies. And the truths hidden inside them, the truth she hadn't seen. "When I told him I had a son, that we were separated, he asked how Jesse was handling it. Said that he understood what it was like to grow up without a father, how difficult it was for a boy."

Ethan's mouth thinned into a straight line. "He didn't say what happened to his father?"

"He claimed he was dead." Rebecca shuddered, remembering the conversation. She'd thought then that Frank's expression was filled with pain. Now she realized that malice had caused the odd flicker in his eyes. And that revenge had been on his mind. He'd planned to take Jesse's father away from him all along.

She shifted and found herself studying Ethan. No matter how much Ethan might have let them down, he would give his life for his son.

Just as she would.

But what if they didn't get the chance?

JESSE BLINKED AND CLENCHED HIS neon wand in one hand as he tried to guess where the car was taking them. Mr. Frank had said they were playing a game, then he'd blindfolded him and told him to play along.

But Jesse didn't like this game. He'd been riding a long time. His stomach growled, and his mouth was dry. So dry it felt like it was stuffed with cotton, kind of like last year when he'd been sick and his mommy had made him drink that cough syrup. His head was fuzzy, too, and it was dark behind the blindfold. So dark he couldn't see a thing.

Being in the dark made everything scarier. The sounds outside were louder: the whine of . other cars, tires screeching, horns honking. People shouting in the streets. A helicopter motor somewhere above.

He'd hoped they were going to another Sox game.

But yesterday it hadn't taken this long to get to Fenway Park. Frog Pond would be all right, too. He wanted to go back and wade.

Sweat trickled down his forehead and rolled beneath the cloth tied around his eyes.

He reached up to tear off the blindfold.

"I don't wanna play anymore," he said.

Mr. Frank slapped his leg. "Don't take off the blindfold, kid."

Jesse swallowed hard. Mr. Frank sounded mad. He'd never called him *kid* before. And he'd never hit him, either.

He sucked in a breath. "I wanna go home. I'm hot, and I'm hungry and tired of this game."

"Shut up," Mr. Frank growled. "We'll be there soon."

"Where are we going?"

But Mr. Frank didn't answer.

Suddenly Jesse felt scared. "Will my mommy be there?"

A nasty laugh boomed through the car as it bounced over a rough patch. "No, kid. Not this time."

"What about my daddy?"

"We might send him a picture," Mr. Frank said with another mean laugh.

"Do you know my daddy?" Jesse asked.

Mr. Frank grunted. "Stop whining."

Jesse bit down on his lip. His mommy never told him to shut up. And neither did his daddy.

He didn't like Mr. Frank right now.

He shoved at the blindfold, determined this time to tear it off. "I wanna go back."

The tires squealed, and the car suddenly swerved off the road and screeched to a stop. Jesse's heart pounded as he pushed at the bindings. Then his car door jerked open, and Mr. Frank suddenly yanked his arm and dragged him out of the car.

"I told you to be quiet, you little brat!"

Jesse's throat clogged with fear. He didn't want to go anywhere with Mr. Frank now. "Let me go," he said, kicking at Mr. Frank. "I'm gonna tell my daddy you was mean to me!"

But Mr. Frank's fingers dug into his arms. "You have no idea how mean I can be, kid."

The sound of the trunk opening made Jesse jerk his head up. Then Mr. Frank picked him up and tossed him inside. He kicked and screamed, but Mr. Frank knocked him backward. Jesse fell against something hard in the trunk. He smelled oil and gas, then heard a loud, dull sound. Mr. Frank had closed the trunk!

Jesse squirmed and struggled and beat against the sides of the car, then at the trunk lid above him. But Mr. Frank didn't come back. The car engine revved, and Jesse was thrown backward as the car bounced over gravel and zoomed back onto the road. Jesse fought tears as he finally pushed off the blindfold. Inside the trunk it was pitch-black.

And he was locked inside with no way to get out.

FINN CURSED A BLUE STREAK AS HE roared through Boston toward the harbor. He had had it with the kid.

Dammit. All those weeks of having to

coach the little brats, putting up with their whiny cries and skinned knees. Pretending like he gave a rat's ass when he would have liked to have snuffed the kid the first time he'd wiped his grimy paws on Finn's clean shirt.

He pulled out his cell phone and punched in his father's number, thumping his hand on the steering wheel as it rang three times. The blackout plaguing the city painted the sky-scrapers in dark shadows, making even the water look muted and gray. A ship's horn wailed above the sound of frustrated drivers and their horns.

Finally, Liam answered. "Is everything going as scheduled?"

Finn laughed. "Yeah. Except I'm ready to do the kid now. Should I shoot him, then dump him in the bay?"

"No." Liam made a disgusted sound in his throat. "Don't be in such a hurry, son. We've waited too long for this to end it so quickly."

Finn's mouth watered for revenge almost as badly as his dad's. But the kid was driving him mad. "What do you want me to do, then?"

"Let's give Ethan a chance to find the boy. Then he can witness his death." Liam chuckled.

"That will be the best part," Finn said. "Watching his face when he sees me put a bullet in the boy's head."

With that sweet image in his mind, he guessed he could stand the kid a while longer, as long as he kept him locked in the trunk. But when he reached their temporary hiding place, if the kid gave him any trouble, he'd find a way to make him be quiet.

His father said he didn't want him dead yet.

But he didn't say Finn couldn't hurt him a little first.

Chapter Six

Jesse had been missing now for two hours. Two hours that felt like a million.

Ethan wiped his brow. The August heat was stifling. Ordinarily he'd look forward to sunset, but not tonight.

"Ethan, I need to leave and help the team track down Liam," Ty said. "We think he has a bigger attack planned."

Ethan nodded. The situation looked bleak. "Damn him to hell, all the Sheas."

Ty clapped him on the back. "Hang in there, Matalon. We'll do everything we can to find Jesse." He cut his eyes toward Rebecca. "You two belong together, you know."

Ethan frowned and glanced at Rebecca. She stood staring out the window, her body rigid with tension. He knew guilt was eating her up inside, but it was his fault their son was missing.

It was his job to protect them.

But he'd failed.

"I let them both down," Ethan said through the knot in his throat.

"It's not over, buddy." Ty's voice sounded gravelly, as well. "We've been through missions before that looked hopeless, and we survived."

But none of them had been as personal as this one. "Don't worry. I'm not giving up," Ethan said. "Far from it. I'll never give up looking for my son."

Ty started toward the door but then hesitated, an odd look on his face.

"What is it?" Ethan asked.

Ty's thick eyebrows bunched together. "I'm still trying to piece together how the Sheas masterminded this plan. They had to have inside help from somewhere."

"What are you thinking?"

Ty shrugged. "I don't know. Hell...I was thinking about this girl I met on the Internet. Wondering if she might be involved." He shook his head. "Guess I'm getting paranoid."

A downfall of every job Ty had had—with Special Forces, the Secret Service and Eclipse. You learned quickly to trust no one but each other.

Just as they all had during that Mideast mission. But something had gone wrong, and all this time they'd believed it had been Liam's fault. What if it hadn't been?

It still didn't give Liam the right to take Jesse.

With that thought nagging at him, Ethan turned back to Ty. "I'm surprised that you're meeting women online, but glad you're getting back out there."

Ty's smile was sad. He'd never recovered from his wife's death. Ethan honestly wondered if Ty would ever get involved with another woman.

"Actually, it started out as an assignment," Ty said. "I've been keeping tabs on Liam Shea for Vice-President Davis the past year, hacking into his site. I noticed someone else hacking in, and my techie did a search and discovered it was a woman from Boston. She frequents other sites as well, including an Internet dating site called Webmatch."

"Let me guess. You set yourself up as her perfect match."

"Exactly." Ty whistled. "If her picture looks anything like her, she's pretty sweet eye candy."

"But you don't trust her."

"I don't trust anyone and you know it," Ty said. "Especially someone I developed a relationship with online."

"Trust your instincts," Ethan said. "If you're wondering about her, check her out."

Ty reached for the doorknob. "I'm already on it."

He walked out the door, and Ethan turned back to business. He couldn't waste time.

His son's life depended on his quick thinking and skills. There would be time to beat himself up later.

REBECCA HAD ONCE LOVED ETHAN'S house, a cream-colored Federal row house with an iron fence at street level, but today as she stepped onto the second-story rear balcony overlooking the courtyard filled with foliage and a wrought-iron bench, the house felt empty and lonely. A baseball lay in a flowerbed, a bat beside it, evidence that Jesse had once played there but was missing today.

She stepped back inside and went to the front window overlooking Louisburg Square, then studied the pedestrians trying to make their way through the stil-crowded, traffic-congested streets. A uniformed policeman herded a group of sweatshirt-hooded teens away from a street corner, obviously suspicious that they were up to no good. Looters had run out from a nearby market earlier. Sirens wailed, whistles blew and horns honked, the tension of the day mounting as those few who'd tried to make it to work attempted to dig their way through the maze of cars and useless traffic lights to get home.

Even Beacon Hill had been touched by the chaos created by the blackout.

She sucked in a sharp breath, then turned and watched the minute hand slowly slide forward, counting off another sixty seconds of waiting, another torturous minute of wondering if her son was all right.

Ethan was on the phone trying to find out more about the Sheas, Finn specifically. She felt helpless, and she hated it.

How could she have let Finn become involved in her son's life? Kiss her? Make her think about a relationship again?

Why hadn't she seen his true motive?

Because you needed to feel loved again.

How pathetic was that?

Ethan hung up the phone, then walked up behind her and started to slide his hands to her arms, but stopped midair and dropped his hands. His anger and accusations hung in the air between them.

She ached to lean into him, but still she blamed him, too. If he'd only told her about the Sheas, warned her that Liam was out of prison. If only he'd been there for her and Jesse.

But Ethan was so driven, had a one-track mind when it came to his software company. Success, millions and a Beacon Hill address were what drove him. And he'd gotten them all. Then there was his work with Eclipse.

She'd tried to understand, but he'd never wanted to talk about the missions afterward, had never confided any of the details.

Sometimes she'd noticed the shadows in his eyes, sensed he was haunted by things he'd done and seen. Yet he'd been as obsessive about continuing as he'd been about his company. He'd shut himself off from her when she'd wanted to listen.

Just as they were both shutting down now. Despite needing comfort, they were both unable to reach for each other.

Ethan could be hard and cold one minute, loving and tender the next. He'd made love like he could never get enough of her, sometimes hard and fast, taking and demanding. But he'd always pleasured her, too.

Her body ached for that kind of connection again.

"Rebecca…" His voice wavered, and he hesitated as if he wanted to say more, but didn't. She couldn't make herself speak, either.

Finally he cleared his throat. "Did Finn— Frank Sullivan—mention some place that he'd go? Maybe a cabin? Another city?"

She shook her head, but another thought struck her, and she reached for her oversize purse, her heart pounding.

"What is it?" Ethan asked.

"My camera. I might have pictures of him in there from one of Jesse's games. Then you can see how he looks now. That might help."

"Let's see."

"Oh, no." She bit down on her lip as she accessed the memory card. "Right before the trip I deleted photos of Jesse's baseball game after I uploaded them onto my home computer."

"Look through what's left," Ethan said. "Maybe you didn't delete them all."

She began to scroll through the photos, her pulse clamoring at a picture of Jesse at the airport wearing his Red Sox jersey.

"God, Ethan, Jesse was so excited about the game. We dropped Frank off at Logan first." Tears pushed at her eyelids as she found one of Jesse holding his mitt in one hand, a ball in the other. They were standing at the taxi stand, but Frank had already gone into the terminal.

She forced herself to scroll forward, then her eyes widened as she noticed Frank in the background of another photo. She and Jesse were waiting for a taxi to go to the game, but in the background Frank was exiting the airport door.

"That's him," she said in a low whisper. "But he's leaving the airport."

Ethan gripped her arm. "See if there are more."

She flipped through a couple more random shots, then noticed Frank near another taxi stand. In the next picture, he was climbing into a cab.

"Let me have it," Ethan said. "I want to see if we can get a license number on the cab and the name of the company."

She handed the camera to him, and he connected it to his computer. Within seconds, he'd uploaded the photos, then used his software to enlarge the picture so they could study the details.

Rebecca narrowed her eyes, trying to read the numbers. He enhanced the picture again, and a partial plate came into view, but he couldn't read the name of the cab company.

"I'm going to run this," Ethan said. "See if we can find the taxi service. Maybe the driver can tell us where he took Frank Sullivan."

Rebecca nodded, twisting her fingers together, hope sparking inside her. This was a clue. She had to hold on to that fact. They were one step closer to finding Jesse.

She only hoped they'd find him before dark.

He was precocious, stubborn, funny, sometimes devilish. So much like his father.

But he was terrified of the dark, and night was coming.

Past stories about other kidnapped children echoed in her head. The terrified parents. The pleas to find their missing children.

She glanced at the clock. Every hour that passed when a child was missing decreased the chances of finding the child alive.

ADRENALINE SURGED through Ethan. Finally a lead. Granted, the partial license plate was a small clue, but at this point, he'd take anything.

He plugged the license number into the database and watched as the software program sorted the information and spilled out several numbers. He narrowed the search to taxi services and located the name of the service within minutes.

On his computer he routed his home phone to his cell. Thank goodness for technology.

He hung up, and because there was no power, e-mailed the photo of Finn Shea/aka Frank Sullivan to his cell phone. "Come on, we're going to find the cab driver who drove Finn from the airport."

Rebecca followed him to the car. "I hope he can tell us something."

Ethan squeezed her arm. "Me, too. At least it's a place to start."

Anything was better than just sitting around on their asses waiting.

Leaving his brownstone and easing onto the clogged street wasn't easy, but Ethan flashed phony professional identification, courtesy of Eclipse, and one of the cops cleared the way. They headed toward East Boston.

The drive to the taxi company dragged, and the sound of a siren screeching made his heart jump to his throat. At a corner, the sight of a man clutching his little boy's hand as they crossed the street made Ethan's chest constrict.

"I keep searching the sidewalks," Rebecca said in a haunted voice. "Thinking I'm going to see him in the crowd, that he'll be there and I'll call his name and he'll come running up…"

Her voice broke, and Ethan couldn't help himself. He laid a hand over hers. There was so much between them. So many memories. So much love. So much pain.

"I know. I keep seeing the awe on his face the first time I took him to a game," Ethan said, his chest aching. "He was only two, but he clapped and waved that little banner you bought him."

"I think he liked baseball so much because it was something you always did with him," Rebecca said.

Except he hadn't shown yesterday. Maybe if he had, if he'd kept Jesse overnight, had been with him today…

They arrived at the taxi company, and he shut off the condemning voice inside his head as he pulled into the parking lot. Rebecca jumped out of the car before he could go around to help her. Together they walked inside, and Ethan waved down the receptionist.

He flashed credentials again. "My name is Ethan Matalon. I'm investigating a kidnapping and need some information."

The woman's eyes widened. "What kidnapping? I haven't seen anything on the news."

"That's because I haven't reported it. It was my son," Ethan said stonily.

"I don't see how I can help you."

"It's about a fare one of your drivers picked up yesterday."

The woman wrinkled her nose and glanced toward the back room. "I don't think we're supposed to give out that information."

Ethan's patience snapped. "Look, ma'am, this is a life-or-death situation."

A burly man wearing grubby coveralls eyed him from the back, and a short stubby man with a bad toupee and a sweat-stained shirt stepped inside. "What's the problem, mister?"

Rebecca caught the man's arm, then explained the situation. "Please, sir, my son's life depends on it."

Her soft plea softened his stern expression, and he gave a clipped nod. "All right. What exactly are you looking for?"

Ethan produced the partial license plate. "I believe the man who kidnapped this child got a ride from the airport yesterday in one of your cabs. Check your log sheets and find out who was driving the car with these plates. I need to speak to him immediately."

The man checked the logbook, then scribbled down a name. Tomas Cunning.

"Is he working today?" Ethan asked.

"No, he didn't show or call, either."

"Can you give me his address and some information about his stops yesterday afternoon?"

Rebecca estimated the time Sullivan had been picked up, and they waited while the manager accessed the information on his laptop.

Over his shoulder Ethan skimmed the data. Cunning had made three drops within a thirty-minute time frame. Damn. Which one had been Finn Shea? He moved over so

Rebecca could see the screen. "Do you recognize any of these stops?"

Rebecca shook her head.

"All right. Come on, we're going to talk to
Mr. Cunning."

They jumped in the car, and Ethan spun
from the parking lot, then drove along the
highway, veering off to the address the
manager had written down. It was a small,
older neighborhood with run-down homes
that were probably rentals. Ethan coasted
through the narrow streets, checking addresses until he located Cunning's, a small
house with faded green paint, a beat-up Pinto
in the drive and a mutt that snarled at them
when they climbed out of the car.

Ethan fended off the dog with a sharp
command, but the hairs on the animal's neck
stood on end as Ethan approached the front
door. Something didn't feel right. He'd experienced the same instinct countless times before
on missions, and it usually meant trouble.

"Ethan?"

"Stay behind me." He pushed Rebecca

backward with one hand and shielded her with his body while he drew his gun.

Slowly he inched forward, the rickety steps creaking as he climbed up onto the porch. The screen door was ripped in several places, the inside door ajar.

Again, that sense that something was wrong tickled his spine. He slowly opened the door and put one foot inside the foyer, but the scent of blood and urine assaulted him.

Another step and he was inside the dark, musty entryway. He spotted a man sprawled on the scarred linoleum floor, one arm bent at an awkward angle as if it was broken, a pool of blood surrounding his head.

Frustration made his throat dry. Dammit, they were too late. Cunning was dead.

He'd taken a bullet to the brain, execution-style.

Finn's work, no doubt. *Leave No Witnesses Behind.*

His gut clenched. He had to find Jesse before Finn killed him, too. Finn wouldn't care that he was just a kid.

He'd simply consider him a casualty for the cause.

But he couldn't share that fact with Rebecca.

LIAM SHEA HOPED THE MEN who'd betrayed him were all suffering.

He stared outside at the sky and smiled at the chaos and violence he'd set into motion. Seeing his plan being orchestrated was a dream come true, one he'd anticipated for years.

One the Special Forces team had not seen coming.

No. They'd each been caught up in their own lives, too busy to notice or worry about him. While he'd rotted in that hellhole of a prison, they'd built careers, lives, and had not once even paid him a visit.

They'd turned their backs on him as if he hadn't been a fearless member of their elite squad. As if he didn't know their dirty secrets.

Today they were paying.

He closed his eyes, letting the hatred heat his blood and fuel his urges to kill as memories of that fatal day rolled through him. The day his life, his family, his career had ended.

He remembered that day as if it were yesterday. The hostage situation had gone on too long. Several countries had made rescue attempts and failed.

Commander Bradley had put together the team. Bradley knew of Liam's grudge against the radical sect who held the hostages. They'd set a car bomb that had damn near killed Liam. But Bradley knew Liam was the best, and Liam had been determined to prove that he could handle the mission.

Raised like the Kennedys, his family had served the U.S. in every conflict since World War I. Liam had been in line to make it to the White House one day. A successful rescue attempt would have won him great favor toward those political aspirations.

But Grant Davis had wanted the same thing as him—to be president. Grant was cunning, conniving and saw Liam as a threat. Still, they'd worked together on the mission. Or so Liam had thought.

Grant had betrayed him in the end, though. He was more certain of it every day.

Sweat rolled down Liam's cheek as he remembered the team moving into position for the rescue.

Grant had maneuvered Liam into an alcove leading to the cavernlike basement where the hostages were being held. Because the captors had scrambled all the frequencies in the building, Bradley had resorted to a visual cue. In the alcove, though, Liam had momentarily lost sight of Bradley. Then he'd seen the cue and had cut the power, plunging the basement into blackness.

But the timing had been off and the mission went bad. Gunfire had exploded. He'd taken a bullet in the chest and collapsed in a pool of his own blood in a deserted stretch of the building.

Liam could still hear the shouts and gunfire, the shouts and cries of the victims subjected to cyanide gas.

Thankfully, the Special Forces team had had masks and had rushed in to get the hostages to clean air. Liam had lost consciousness for a few seconds, then had awakened and thought his men had left him to die. Then Grant Davis had appeared. At first, he'd thought Grant wasn't going to help him, that maybe he had shot him in the dark, but he couldn't be sure. Then voices had echoed nearby, and Davis had helped him out.

Grant Davis had been named a hero for saving him and the hostages to whom he'd administered the antidote.

No one had wanted to hear Liam's side. Instead, they'd court-martialed him for disobeying orders.

Secretary of State Rollins had been one of the unlucky hostages. Because of his emphysema, he hadn't survived the cyanide gas. Liam always believed his sentence had been worse because of the man's death.

After he went to prison his wife had left him. His sons had been shamed.

And he had relived that mission every day for years. His hatred for the men he'd once considered his band of brothers mounted with every second. As did his suspicions.

He had no doubt Grant Davis had purposely maneuvered him into that alcove that day, tricked him to believing his signal was Commander Bradley's. And Davis would have left him to die if footsteps hadn't sounded nearby.

Now they all had to suffer.

Ethan had to know how it felt to lose a son.

Then Grant Davis would know how it felt to lose everything, just as Liam had years ago.

Chapter Seven

Rebecca stared at the cabbie's body in stunned silence. Blood and brain matter had splattered on the walls and floor. Mingling with the scent of mold and beer, the stench of death and body wastes filled the air.

A cold numbness spread through her as she realized that the man who'd done this was the same man who had kidnapped her son.

The type of man who killed in cold blood.

Horrified, she backed against the wall. "God, Ethan. I can't believe Frank did this."

"Finn," Ethan clarified coldly.

And now that this man was dead, they'd lost their only lead. Despair robbed her of air, which she released on a sob.

Ethan grabbed her and pulled her out of sight of the body, then shook her gently.

"Shh, Bec, shh."

"But this man could have told us where Frank went and—"

Ethan suddenly pressed his mouth to hers, stroking her arms as he kissed her. "It's all right. We'll find another way."

She clung to his arms, shaking uncontrollably.

Ethan traced a finger along her cheek. "You have to be strong now, Bec."

She nodded, gulping back more tears. Ethan's eyes were glazed with emotions, his body tight with tension. Whether or not he wanted to admit it, he was scared, too.

Affection and tenderness for him mushroomed inside her, making her momentarily forget that this was partly his fault.

And her own.

All she knew was that she needed Ethan now. She arched her head and kissed him this time, desperate to feel him against her, to assuage the fear and pain seeping through her.

He moaned as if he was hurting as well,

and the kiss that started out tentative erupted into something much more potent as he plunged his tongue inside her mouth and poured his own frustration and hunger into the moment.

Outside, a car engine sounded, and Ethan abruptly released her, yanking her away from the window as he peered outside.

"Damn. A neighbor just drove by. We have to get out of here."

She reached for the wall to steady herself, but Ethan grabbed her hand. "Don't touch anything." He tugged her back out the front door. "Come on, let's hurry in case the neighbor gets suspicious and returns."

"But we need to call the police," Rebecca whispered.

"No." Ethan spun her toward him, then cupped her face between his hands. "If we call them now, we'll have to stay and talk to them, explain why we're here."

Oh, God. Rebecca trembled. Finn Shea had warned them not to call the police.

The same blue Toyota rolled past the drive, and Ethan clutched Rebecca's hand. "He's back. He must know Cunning. Get in the car. Pretend like nothing's wrong."

"I hate to just leave Mr. Cunning here…"

"We will report his death," Ethan said. "But we have to find Jesse first."

He was right.

The man in the Toyota slowed and stared at them, and she thought he was going to stop. Although her legs threatened to buckle, she tucked her hand around Ethan's arm and forced a smile. Her cheeks ached with the effort, but she huddled next to Ethan and walked to the car as if they were a couple who had just come to visit, not frantic parents of a kidnapped boy who had discovered the only man who might lead them to the kidnapper murdered in cold blood.

The poor man. He had been a simple taxi driver. Had nothing to do with Finn Shea or his father, yet Finn had killed him anyway.

Which meant he would have no qualms killing Jesse.

A shudder tore through her as they climbed in the car, and Ethan started the engine. He pulled out into the street, then checked the rearview mirror as they neared the corner in the bend.

"Damn. The guy is pulling into Cunning's drive. We'd better get the hell out of here."

Ethan punched the gas and sped up, racing away. She held on to the seat, her nerves on edge as they fled the dead man's house.

"Where are we going now?" Rebecca asked as she looked over her shoulder.

Ethan's expression remained grim, but he held up the paper on which he'd jotted the addresses they'd obtained at the cab office, then veered back onto the road toward Logan Airport. "We have three places to check out. But first we're going to switch cars."

Rebecca frowned. "Why?"

"Because once that guy back there calls the police, they may start looking for us."

Then they would be charged with leaving the scene of a crime, or perhaps with murder.

ETHAN BATTLED PANIC AS HE SPED through the tunnel toward Logan Airport. A siren wailed from a police car heading the opposite way, toward Cunning's house, and he increased his speed again, anger at Finn stirring his blood.

If he'd already hurt Jesse…

No. Liam wanted revenge. And so did Finn. They'd probably keep Jesse alive just long enough to torment him. Maybe they wanted him to find them so he could watch them kill his son.

As sick and twisted as that possibility sounded, he latched on to hope. Anything to keep his son alive long enough to save him.…

The signs for the airport slid into view. He took the turn to the long-term parking and maneuvered his way through the lanes until he located a parking spot. He and Rebecca climbed out, walked to the terminal and hopped a shuttle to the car rental place. A few minutes later, he drove away in a black Lexus coupé, grateful for the tinted windows.

"Let's check out the address in the North End first."

Rebecca nodded, twisting her hands in her lap while they headed to Boston's version of "Little Italy." The oldest neighborhood in the city boasted narrow cobblestone streets with multistoried apartment houses and tiny homes. He passed the Old North Church and Copp's Hill Burial Ground that overlooked the Charles River. He'd been here many times during the weekly Italian feasts and the summer festivals.

Jesse had liked the ethnic foods and parades. He'd also enjoyed watching the ships on the river. Ethan had promised him a trip to the seaport district to tour some of the old vessels, but he hadn't followed through.

His heart clenched. He just prayed he had the opportunity to do so. Emotions clouded his throat, and he swallowed hard. It would be the first excursion he'd plan when he brought his son home. And he'd never miss another Red Sox game again.

He glanced at Rebecca and imagined the three of them at the game together. And on other trips. A day in Chinatown. Picnics at the park. Walking on the beach.

Back at Cunning's she had let him kiss her and comfort her, but she'd been in shock. When this was over, would she hate him for the trauma their son had suffered? Would she still want that divorce, or would she give him another chance?

Did he want that chance?

He reached the address on the cab company stationery, and veered into the street in front of the small house. It wasn't showy and ostentatious like the kind of home he expected Finn to buy, too family oriented.

Which made it a great place to hide and blend in with a kidnapped child.

He parked and angled his head toward Rebecca. "You want to wait in the car?"

"No, I'm going with you."

He nodded, and they got out and walked up to the door together. He knocked on the door, tensing when he heard footsteps. A child's voice echoed from behind the doorway. A little boy's. He was crying.

Ethan pulled his gun, and pressed Rebecca behind him. The door swung open to reveal a short round woman with thick black hair. She muttered a string of words in Italian, her eyes widening at the sight of the gun.

She didn't look like she'd work for Finn, but then again, he could have hired her to take care of Jesse temporarily.

He flashed his identification, then the cell phone picture of Frank Sullivan/Finn. "I'm looking for this man. Have you seen him?"

"No," the woman snapped. "Now put away that gun. You'll scare my grandson."

He pushed his way past her. "Let me see the boy."

"You can't come in here!" the woman shouted. "Sal, call the police!"

Rebecca grabbed her arm. "Please," she pleaded. "My son is missing. The taxi driver had this address listed for a man he dropped off—the man we think is the kidnapper. We have to make sure he's not here."

A black-haired, pudgy boy around seven rounded the corner, rubbing at red swollen eyes. Ethan hesitated, and lowered the gun to his side.

"What's wrong, son?" Ethan asked.

"I stubbed my toe." As if to prove his point, the boy stuck out his foot to reveal a puffy big toe that had been bleeding.

"He didn't want me to clean it," the grand-mother answered.

"I'm sorry, ma'am." Ethan backed away, pulling Rebecca with him. "My mistake."

Dammit.

He'd wanted the kid to be Jesse so bad he'd almost lost control.

Frustrated, he rushed back to the car and silently climbed in, wiping sweat from his brow. Rebecca's face showed strain, and tension filled the car as they drove to the next address on the list, Chinatown.

Ethan's gut told him this was a dead end, but he had to check any possible lead. The drop-off address was a restaurant, and when he and Rebecca went inside, the group of Chinese people looked at him with disdain.

He showed the photo of Frank/Finn anyway, but each of the staff and guests he asked simply shook their heads.

Rebecca sighed as they hurried to the car and drove to the last address. "This has to be it."

Her breath rattled in the quiet that had settled between them as he neared Back Bay, one of the most desirable neighborhoods in Boston.

The brownstones were beautiful, more to Finn's taste, Ethan thought.

Did Finn live in one of them? Had he bought a home here so he could spy on Ethan and execute his father's plan?

He squeezed Rebecca's hand and they made their way up the flower-lined sidewalk to the front door of the address they sought. But he sensed in his gut that this was a dead end, too.

Then what would he do?

The door opened a few seconds later, and a yuppie-looking couple greeted them, arms entwined. "How can we help you?" the man asked.

Ethan went through the motions, but it was obvious this couple was not working for Finn.

"I thought we were on to something," Rebecca said after they thanked the couple and settled back in the car. "But he could be anywhere, Ethan. He might have taken Jesse out of the city, even out of the country."

"I don't think so," Ethan said. "Finn is setting a trap for me. If I don't find him, he loses out on seeing me hurt."

Something niggled at the back of his mind,

and he punched in the number of the cab company and requested to speak to the manager. "Listen. Check your computer, see if there could have been an address deleted." He explained how to access the deleted files and seconds later, hung up the phone, his hand shaking.

"What is it?" Rebecca asked in a strained voice.

Ethan swallowed hard. "There was one other address." He couldn't believe it. Finn had been right under his nose.

"Where?"

Ethan started the car, his temper firing his blood. "Beacon Hill," he muttered with a curse. "The bastard has been living three doors down from me and I didn't even know it."

REBECCA WATCHED QUIETLY AS Ethan pounded on the door of the brownstone three doors down from his own. Anger and self-condemnation radiated from him. There was nothing she could do to assuage his temper or guilt, because she understood it too well. She was plagued with guilt herself.

After two attempts, Ethan began to pick the lock. Judging from the deft way he maneuvered the small tool in his hand, he'd broken into other places before. She strategically placed herself at an angle to cover him from any passersby, smiling at an elderly couple who studied them anxiously. The blackout had everyone on edge, and so far there were no signs that the lights would be restored anytime soon.

The door lock clicked, and Ethan darted a glance around the street, then inched inside. She stepped into the foyer behind him, her breath tight in her chest. They were breaking and entering.

What if they had the wrong house again? What if they burst in on a family upstairs?

"Stay here—let me see if it's clear." Ethan drew his gun and swept the downstairs, but there was no one, no evidence of Finn or a child.

She waited in the foyer for him to check the upstairs rooms, her gaze skimming what she could see of the first floor. At first glance, the brownstone's layout mirrored Ethan's, yet the furnishings were bare-bones; a black leather sofa in the den along with a plasma TV and a coffee table. The adjacent kitchen looked stark and nearly empty, housing a simple glass-topped table and chairs and a coffeemaker. There were no pictures on the walls, no homey accents, no personal items of any kind.

No note telling them where to find Jesse.

She stepped into the kitchen and checked the refrigerator. If there was food here, Finn might return. A box with leftover pizza and a shriveled orange were the only contents.

Ethan came up behind her, startling her. She hadn't heard him walk down the stairs. He moved like that on missions, she realized, stealthily so he could slip in and out of places without being detected.

"Is this the right address?" she asked.

Anger and some other emotion darkened his eyes. "Yes."

She clutched his arm, bracing herself for bad news. "What is it, Ethan? What did you find?"

His expression held concern and a grimness she'd never seen before.

"Jesse? God, Ethan, tell me. Is he here?"

"No." Ethan took her hands in his. "But this is Finn's place. Upstairs, the office…"

"What?" She jerked away and ran up the stairs. She had to know the truth.

She froze at the entrance to the bedroom Finn had used as an office, bile rising to her throat. The walls were covered with photographs of her, Jesse and Ethan. Swallowing back her emotions, she forced her feet forward, studying the sick display. Pictures of the two of them together dated back to their early marriage. The more recent photos of Ethan and Jesse at Boston Common, of her and Jesse skating on Frog Pond, the three of them at a Red Sox game, shots of Ethan jogging, of him at his brownstone, of them attending Trinity Church for a Christmas service. Another section detailed her life in L.A. There were shots of her entering the TV station, her house, the market, shots of her and Jesse at the beach, in her backyard, inside her house.

She pivoted and saw another section, horror striking her. These photos were much more lewd. They captured her inside her house, in her bedroom undressing, crawling into bed, in her bathroom stripping, then naked in the shower. Dozens of shots taken at different times of the day, of the year.

"Oh my God…" Her knees buckled, and Ethan caught her. "How did he get those?"

Ethan's jaw clenched. "The bastard must have installed cameras in your house."

Her skin crawled as if Finn had actually touched her. The thought of him viewing her private moments, of knowing that he'd been stalking her all those months, watching her undress, bathe, made her feel violated in a way that she'd never felt before.

Head spinning, she turned and ran for the stairs, but Ethan caught her in the doorway and swept her in his arms. Sobs racked her as anger churned through her. "I hate him," she cried. "I hate him for taking Jesse, and I hate myself for letting him get near either one of us."

"I know, baby, I know," Ethan crooned. "But listen to me, Bec. Finn Shea will pay for this, I promise. I will save Jesse, then I'll kill Finn with my bare hands."

Her cell phone rang, jarring them both apart, and she jerked her gaze to Ethan.

"See who it is," he said.

She checked the number. "It says out of area."

"Answer it," Ethan said, leaning closer so he could hear the caller, as well.

She clicked to receive the call. "Hello."

"How do you like my artwork, Rebecca?"

A chill engulfed her at the sound of Frank Sullivan's gritty voice. But he wasn't Frank, he was Finn. He'd lied and used and violated her in so many ways.

"You're a sick bastard," she whispered hoarsely. "Where is my son?"

"He's all tied up for now." Finn barked a laugh. "But aren't you honored that I've devoted an entire wall to you?"

"Tell me what you want," Rebecca ground out. "I'll give you anything, just don't hurt Jesse."

He tsked. "Just knowing Matalon is suffering, that he's seen the pictures I took of you in the shower, that pleases me for now."

"Let me speak to Jesse!" Rebecca shouted.

Ethan grabbed the phone. "Listen to me, you bastard, it's me you want, not Jesse. Tell me where to meet you, and we'll make a trade."

"My father and I have waited years for this moment," Finn snarled. "Don't think it's going to be that easy, Matalon. You have to be punished."

Ethan cursed, but the phone clicked into silence.

Rebecca's heart hammered in her chest as she waited, the sound of Finn's voice echoed in her head. He was laughing at her, had enjoyed making her squirm.

And he knew they were here now.

How?

She raced toward the window, searching the street, hunting for a car abandoned along the road, a stranger lurking nearby, Finn standing in the shadows gloating over his evil plan. But nothing stood out.

Perspiration made her hands clammy as she peered down the street, at the brownstones across the road, checking the windows. Shadows streaked the glass, a feeling of foreboding overwhelming her.

Where the hell was he? And how long would he torment them with his sick game before letting them know if Jesse was still alive, or if he'd already killed him?

JESSE SQUEEZED THE NEON WAND in his fist, holding on to it for dear life as the car bounced and swerved on the road. Where was Mr. Frank taking him? Was he still in Boston or anywhere near his hotel?

He'd managed to tear off the stupid blindfold, but he still hadn't been able to see. He had no idea how long the wand would work, so he'd forced himself to turn it off. But he hated the dark, and he had to flick it on every few minutes just to remind himself that there weren't any monsters in the trunk with him.

There was one driving the car, though. Mr. Frank. He was big and mean, and Jesse wanted to see his mommy and tell her that he was a bad man.

The car bounced over another rut, then slammed to a stop. Jesse tried to listen, to figure out where he was, but all he could hear was his own breathing rattling in the dark. He was so scared he thought he was going to pee his pants.

Suddenly, the trunk door lifted open, and Jesse squinted in the light. Then a shadow loomed over him. Mean Mr. Frank.

Jesse coughed, trying to be brave. "You gonna let me go now?"

"Not yet, kid. I've got a party planned first."

A party? His voice didn't sound like it would be a fun kind of party. Not one Jesse wanted to go to. He was hot and scared and wanted his mommy and daddy.

But he had a feeling he'd better play along. "What kind of party?"

"A surprise one for your daddy."

Jesse's heart thundered. Mr. Frank said the word *daddy* like it was a bad word. And it wasn't his daddy's birthday so why would he have a party? "Can I see my mommy then?"

Mr. Frank's mean laugh rumbled out. Then Jesse heard the sound of a big truck, then another truck's engine, and frowned. Where were they? Not at someone's house…

Mr. Frank suddenly reached down and pulled a big burlap bag from the trunk. Jesse had been lying on it, and his body tumbled sideways. Then Mr. Frank jerked him up and tried to shove the bag over his head.

"No! Stop it!" Jesse shoved at the bag, but Mr. Frank knocked him backward with a hand across his face. Stars swam in the darkness, and Jesse reached up to rub his head and felt blood.

Mr. Frank grabbed his arm and jammed the bag over his head, then pushed at his feet to cram them inside. Jesse shouted and kicked and tried to punch him, but he couldn't fight him off.

Then Mr. Frank picked him up and threw him over his shoulder like a sack of potatoes. Jesse's head spun as he bobbed against the man's big body. His heavy footsteps pounded something hard. Metal. Like steps. More footsteps pounded on some floor that sounded hollow. Was he inside one of the big trucks?

A minute later, Mr. Frank tossed him onto the floor, and pain rolled through his arm and shoulder. Jesse heard the door screech and slam shut. He struggled and kicked, desperate to get out of the bag. The material scratched his arms and legs, and sweat poured down his face. He gagged, trying to breathe, but he was choking. The bag smelled funny and it clawed at his skin.

He wiggled his feet and managed to slide one through the bag's opening. It took him forever, but he squirmed and wiggled and kicked and fought until he tore the bag off his head. The place was so dark he couldn't see his own hands.

But he felt around him, reached for the walls, and beat against them, yelling for someone to let him out. His voice sounded tiny and hollow, and he wondered if anyone could hear him.

Fighting panic, he flipped on his lighted wand, and shined it around, searching for a way to escape. But he was in the back of some kind of cargo truck. He crawled around the edge and beat against it with his fists until his hands hurt, and his throat was raw. But no one came.

Finally, he dropped his head and gulped, hot tears dribbling down his face. He was alone with no way to get out. His mommy and daddy didn't know where he was.

And he had a bad feeling that Mr. Frank wasn't going to come back and get him. That he was going to let him rot in here.

He clenched the wand tighter. What if the light burned out? Or the air? He'd seen a movie once where bad men carried illegal immigrants in the back of a big truck and left them. By the time the cops found them, they were dead.

What if he died in here in the dark and no one ever found him?

Chapter Eight

Finn cursed as he strode back to his car. Thankfully, he'd found the old abandoned warehouses on the outside of town. The truck was the perfect temporary hiding spot. There was no one even remotely nearby the warehouse, so Jesse Matalon could scream his freaking head off and no one would hear.

The sound of Rebecca's horrified voice filled his head, and made his blood pump faster. He still wished he had time to bed her, to make Matalon watch him with his precious wife, before he killed their son and the two of them.

The night air rejuvenated him, and reminded him of the seaport district where he'd eventually take the boy. When he was little, his father had taken him fishing. They would have enjoyed a lot more family excursions if the men of the Special Forces team hadn't betrayed his dad and sent him to prison.

His cell phone vibrated, and he checked the number as he started the engine. He was going to grab something to eat, maybe a beer, wait a while before he instigated the next phase of his plan.

"Hello."

"Finn, how's it going?" Liam asked.

"Everything's right on schedule."

"Where's the boy?"

"Right now I've got him stuffed in an old truck at an abandoned warehouse near the airport."

"Did anyone see you?"

"No, Dad," Finn said irritably. "It's completely deserted."

"Have you contacted Matalon?"

"I sent him a message. But I haven't set up the final showdown. Figured I'd let him sweat a while longer." He paused, lit a cigarette. "He finally figured out that I've been staying down the street." He smiled as he thought about Ethan discovering the photographs of Jesse and Rebecca. Especially those nudes of Rebecca. She hadn't realized how many satisfying nights she'd given him during his private peep show.

Liam laughed. "Revenge is sweet, isn't it?"

"Damn right. I remember when we first got together to discuss our plans. It seems like yesterday."

"Not for me." Liam heaved a sigh. "There were times I thought I'd never be released from that hellhole."

"I know it was hard, Dad. But Grant Davis will finally pay for betraying you."

He had to. He'd stolen his father's life. Finn's and his brother's, as well. Hatred coiled inside Finn like a viper needing to strike. Grant Davis hadn't deserved to be dubbed a hero while his father sat in a cell. And Davis sure as hell didn't deserve to be in public office now, gloating over his political career—the career his father should have had.

Finn remembered the first time they'd talked about revenge back when his father was behind bars. He'd been in his late teens, angry and eager to do something to have his father back.

His mother had completely turned her back on him just like everyone else. But Finn and his brothers worshipped their father, and had hitched a ride to the prison.

The sight of the metal fence and armed guards surrounding the prison had made Finn's stomach knot. He was a rebel himself and couldn't imagine being locked in a small cell like a caged animal. The image of his father wearing that prison uniform had roused his temper to the boiling point. And the handcuffs and chains around his dad's ankles…

He balled his hands into fists, the memory making him antsy to kill Matalon.

That day Liam had calmly relayed the story of the failed mission. He'd insisted that one of his teammates had been responsible for their rescue attempt going awry. Yet Liam was chained like a damn dog while the other men all went free. After endless days of re-playing the details in his mind, he'd settled on Grant Davis. The Georgian had political aspirations, and Liam knew he didn't want the competition from a Shea. Liam and his sons had met and vowed to get back at all the bastards who ruined their lives.

Later, when his father had been released and gone to Washington State, every time he'd seen Grant Davis on TV campaigning as the vice-presidential candidate beside Allan Stack, Liam had steamed. And so had Finn.

His father should have been sitting in office, not Grant Davis.

"Just give me the word when you want me to off the kid," Finn said.

His father's growl confirmed that he'd been reliving the past, as well. "Soon, son, soon."

Finn grinned as he pictured the perfect ending.

Matalon tormented as he watched his son die, then Ethan on his knees waiting for Finn to put the bullet in his brain.

ETHAN HAD NEVER HATED ANYONE as passionately as he hated Finn Shea. The man's twisted need for revenge ran as deep as his father's. But as much as Ethan wanted to howl and pound his fist through the man's walls, he had to maintain control.

His son's life depended on his training, on his being focused.

Rebecca's agitated voice drove him from his own tormented thoughts, and he hurried to the window to search the shadows outside. Had Rebecca spotted someone watching them? "What is it, Bec?"

"The call... He knows we're here."

Ethan nodded. "He's either watching or has someone else watching us."

"But I don't see anyone," Rebecca said in a ragged whisper.

Neither did he, but Finn knew how to live in the shadows. Then again, Ethan remembered the photos and whirled around, searching the room. "Cameras," he growled. "He's installed them in his house so he could watch our reactions when we discovered his little photo gallery."

Rebecca paled even more, then narrowed her eyes as she spotted one of the cameras tucked in the corner of a bookcase. "You're right." She stepped forward, angling her head at the camera. "We're going to find you," she shouted. "And if you've hurt my son, I'll kill you myself."

Ethan coaxed Rebecca into a chair away from the photos, then leaned near her ear, telling her to whisper so Finn couldn't hear their conversation. "Rebecca, I'll make it all right. I swear."

She nodded, her eyes glazed. "I can't believe he's so cruel, that he was stalking me for months and I didn't realize it. That he's still watching us now." She glared at the camera. "What a fool…"

Hatred was indeed a strong motivator. "Shh, stop it." He cupped her face between his hands and forced her to look at him, his body vibrating with tension. "Finn probably had help from his father and brothers. Liam Shea was a mastermind, experienced in special ops. He knows how to set up surveillance without being detected."

"But all those cameras in my house. And now here." She shuddered and he rubbed her arms to warm her.

"Listen, Bec, put it out of your mind. He'll

pay, I promise. But right now we have to focus on finding Jesse."

She clamped her teeth over her lower lip. "I know, but how? The cab driver is dead. And Finn is toying with us."

"You're right," Ethan said. "He wants to drag out the chase." Which meant he might have left clues behind. "Let me look around here." He stroked her cheek with the pad of his thumb. "I'm going to call in some favors. Get his phone records. Maybe I can trace him back to Liam."

Dragging in air, Rebecca pushed to her feet. "I want to help."

"Good. Go downstairs, search the drawers in the kitchen. See if you can find a personal planner, date book, anything that might help."

She inhaled again, and he squeezed her arms, grateful to see some color returning to her cheeks. Rebecca was smart, independent and courageous. Seeing her vulnerable, blaming herself ripped at his heart.

He turned to the desk and workstation, holding the last set of photos as she made her way down the stairs to check the kitchen. His eyes drifted to the pictures, and renewed anger swelled inside him, threatening to cut off his oxygen.

He jerked down the nude photos, determined not to let anyone else see them, then stuffed them in a manila envelope and jammed them inside his jacket.

Then he stepped into the hall bathroom and checked it for bugs or a camera. When he found it clean, he phoned Dana, relayed the telephone number on the house phone, then asked her to get addresses and names for any numbers Finn had contacted and to send them to his computer.

"Also, check and see if you can find vehicle registrations for Finn Shea or Frank Sullivan."

"Actually I've already done that for all of the Sheas," Dana said.

"Did you find a car Finn bought here in Boston?"

"Yes. A black Mercedes. 2006." She recited the license number. "Ty has friends on the police force who are looking for those vehicles now."

"Let me know if you track it down."

She agreed, and he hung up, returned to the study and searched the desk. Damn, he wished Finn had a computer here, but Finn was too cunning to make it that easy for him.

Inside the desk, Ethan found meticulous notes detailing Ethan's activities over the past year, proving the Sheas had been keeping an eye on him for months. There was also a notebook filled with notes on Rebecca. Details of her life, where she shopped, restaurants she frequented, meetings and activities. He felt like a voyeur himself just reading them. But he couldn't help his curiosity over what she'd been doing the past year.

Just as he remembered, she liked Thai food. She'd also taken a Chinese cooking class, attended an art gallery opening for a woman named Annika with whom she'd shared several lunches. She had covered countless stories for the news station where she worked.

Of course, he knew most of them because he had watched her. Not only was she spectacular and a natural in front of the camera, but her reporting style was honest, thorough and moving. She'd done an exceptional job on a story about the women suffering in Afghanistan, and had covered several charities, as well as a huge architectural project underway in L.A.

Ethan was happy for her; she'd made her dream to be a journalist come true. Too bad he hadn't supported her more, early in their marriage. She might have made it at a Boston network instead.

He looked again at the notebook. In the margins, Finn had scribbled notes on her appearance, including lascivious remarks about his desire to have her in his bed. He also intended for Ethan to know that he'd taken Ethan's wife as his lover.

His hands curled into fists, his mind traveling down that dangerous road. Had she slept with Finn Shea?

Ethan forced himself to skim on, hoping to find references to places in Boston he might take Jesse, but found nothing. Muttering a curse, he laid the book down and dug deeper in the desk. No checkbook, bank statements, passport, plane tickets or information on his brothers or father…

Damn.

His blood hot with rage, he slammed the drawer shut and moved to the bottom one. When he opened it, he noticed a bundle of maps of Boston and the surrounding area. His pulse clamored as he spread them out.

Several points on the map were circled. The airport, the John Hancock Tower, the hospital where Lily had worked, Boston Common, Chinatown, Cambridge, some abandoned warehouses on the outskirts of town. Some of these places had already been targets.

What about the others? Ty was busy searching for the vice-president and he had someone checking the airports and bus terminals. But after seeing Finn's notes, Ethan sensed Finn had Jesse somewhere nearby. He'd probably used his car or a rental. Maybe he was hiding out in one of those warehouses....

His cell phone vibrated and he grabbed it. "Matalon."

"Ethan, it's Dana. Listen, they found Finn Shea's Mercedes. It's parked at a warehouse in the Marine Industrial Park."

"I'm on my way."

REBECCA FELT AS IF SHE WAS holding her breath as they drove back toward the industrial park. Several warehouses finally appeared, but they bypassed those in search of an abandoned set where Finn's car had been spotted. Several large trucks zoomed from the functioning warehouses, and she jerked her head toward each one, checking out the driver, wondering if her son might possibly be in the back of one of those vehicles. There was such a large area to search. It would be impossible to cover it by themselves.

She gripped her sweating hands together as they passed a police car heading the opposite direction.

"Ethan, maybe we should call in the police. All these warehouses, the trucks. Finn could have stowed Jesse in any one of them."

"No cops," Ethan snapped. "I know the Sheas. We have to play by their rules."

"But Jesse could be anywhere."

Ethan cut his eyes toward her, fear and sympathy mingled in his dark brown gaze. "Hang in there, Rebecca. Try to think about the fun times we had. The things we'll do when we take Jesse home."

Home? Where would that be?

She squeezed her eyes closed, then opened them again, summoning her courage. "He loves the beach and the ocean," she whispered. "Last summer he started a shell collection. He has over one hundred shells now."

"He told me about them when he was here last," Ethan replied. "He said he has them displayed on a board in his room."

"He likes to make sand sculptures, too," Rebecca said, her throat tight. "He still talks about that shark you made with him two years ago." That was right after she'd moved to L.A. and Ethan had come for a visit. She'd just accepted her job at the station, and was uncertain of their future. Although she and Ethan had grown apart, she'd still hoped they might work things out. But time kept passing and the distance between them had grown wider.

She saw her son's face in her mind and clenched her hands. Jesse had missed his father, had cried when Ethan left that day.

She'd been so angry with Ethan she had refused to answer his calls for a week.

What would happen when they found Jesse? Would they sign those divorce papers and go their separate ways?

"I promised I'd teach him to sail." Ethan's throat worked as he swallowed. "I'm going to take some time off and do that this summer."

She wondered if he would or if that was another promise that, albeit made with good intentions, would be broken. Still, she forced a smile, although her cheeks ached with the effort. "He's been talking about that a lot lately. That and his next birthday." She hesitated, praying he would live to celebrate another year. "He wants a Sox party. He asked me if you could arrange for one of the players to come and sign autographs."

Ethan looked pained. "I'll do my damnedest to make that happen."

He clenched the steering wheel and sped up. "There, by that warehouse. I see Finn's car."

Her heart jumped in her chest as he raced toward it, then spun sideways and parked on the side of the street. His hand went to his gun, and he motioned for her to wait while he checked.

"But, Ethan—"

"It might be a trap," he said between gritted teeth. "For all we know, he might have rigged the car to explode."

And kill them before they found Jesse. Oh, God…

She twisted her hands together while he slowly climbed out, surveying the area surrounding the car and the warehouse as he approached. He glanced inside, seemed to be sizing up the situation.

She pressed the window button, and the glass slid down. "Do you see anything of Jesse's?"

Ethan shook his head, then knelt on the ground and looked underneath the vehicle, obviously searching for a device of some kind. A long minute later, he stood, opened the front and examined the engine.

Finally, he turned back to her. "So far, it looks clean. Let me examine the trunk."

In spite of his warning, she couldn't wait inside the stifling car. She had to see. There had to be something inside to indicate Jesse had been in the car, where Finn had taken him from there.

That he was still alive.

But when she glanced over Ethan's shoulder into the dark trunk, panic splintered her chest.

Blood stained the floorboard. Blood that was wet, meaning it was fresh.

Blood that was probably Jesse's.

Chapter Nine

5:00 p.m.

Ethan's heart hammered in his chest at the sight of the blood. It was Jesse's; he knew it in his gut.

All this time, he'd prayed that Finn wouldn't hurt his son, that he had some humanity left and wouldn't actually inflict pain on his little boy, but now he knew different. The cold reality that slapped him in his face spiked his blood to boiling.

He would see that Finn Shea suffered for this.

"Ethan…"

Jerking his head sideways, he noticed all the color drain from Rebecca's face.

She clutched his hand, and he folded her in his arms and held her. "I know it looks bad, but it might not be Jesse's blood."

She shuddered against him, and he stroked her back. But she pummeled her fists on his chest. "He hurt him, Ethan. He hurt our baby."

"Rebecca, shh, maybe it's not Jesse's."

"You don't believe that," she said, hysteria lacing her voice. "You know he's done something awful to him."

Ethan stroked her gently. "Stop it, Bec. Even if it is Jesse's blood, there's not that much of it. He might have just scraped himself or something. I'm going to take samples and have it tested for a match."

"But he was locked in that dark trunk…" Her voice broke, and his gut clenched. His little boy hated the dark and had been thrown into the trunk by a cold bastard.

Memories surfaced of his own traumatic ordeal when he was four, and he hugged Rebecca tighter, needing her as much as she needed him.

He'd owned a little black puppy named Trouble. He wasn't supposed to take him outside by himself, but he thought he was so big, he had snuck out to walk the little guy. But he'd seen a firefly and chased it, and Trouble had slipped away from him. He'd panicked. He had to find the dog. He couldn't let anything happen to his new buddy.

Later, he realized he should have gone inside for his parents, but his mother had argued against having a dog, had said he wasn't responsible enough for a pet. He'd insisted that he was, had begged and pleaded. His daddy was gone. He was the man of the house. He had to prove himself.

Then it had started raining. The sky had been so black he could hardly see his feet in front of him. Thunder had rumbled, and lightning had flashed like fire across the tops of the thick trees. He'd thought he'd spotted Trouble waddling into the storm drain. Ethan had knelt and yelled for the dog, but he hadn't come back, so he'd crawled inside to get him.

Then the skies had opened up with a downpour that had washed the embankment away. Mud and rocks had tumbled down, clogging the opening to the drain.

Ethan had been trapped. The wind had howled and rain had pounded the earth and pipe. He'd seen shadows, monsters inside, had heard them all around him. He'd known they were hovering over the drain ready to grab him if he ever escaped.

Then he'd heard the puppy whimper, and he had pulled himself together. He'd dug his way out and saved his little buddy.

Ethan jerked back to the present, shaking with the memory. He had saved his puppy, and he had to save his son now.

When he'd been trapped, he'd heard his mother's voice echoing in his head, remembered his father's voice when he'd been alive. His father telling him to be brave. Jesse was all alone. Could he hear his parents' voices in his head? Did Jesse even know they were searching for him?

Jesse had begged for a dog the last time he'd visited. If—no, *when* they found him, that was another thing he'd do. He and his son would buy a damn dog.

"Ethan?"

He realized he'd been clenching Rebecca

so tightly she couldn't breathe. Her tender lips brushed his cheek, his neck, then she traced her fingers over his jaw. "Are you all right?" she whispered.

He shook his head. "No, but I will be once we find our son."

Knowing he was wasting time, he pulled away, then tore the bloodied carpet mat from the trunk and carried it to his car. Soon they would know for sure if it was Jesse's.

And if it was, Finn's blood would be the next to spill.

REBECCA TRIED TO CALM HER raging emotions as Ethan searched the car. The way he'd shuddered against her suggested he was just as worried as she was.

She didn't want him beating himself up, yet she knew they both were. How could they not?

Jesse was five. An innocent little boy who'd been caught in a web of sadistic revenge because of his father's past and his mother's idiocy.

How would they go on if they didn't find Jesse alive?

"There's nothing here," Ethan said. "But let's check the warehouse."

She nodded and followed him to the big metal structure that had obviously once provided storage for some kind of company. The minute they entered, she smelled gasoline, along with grease, sweat and cigarette smoke.

The building hadn't been empty for long.

Another odor permeated the air, and she frowned, trying to distinguish the scent. The smell of the sea? Fish?

Had the company transported seafood? Perhaps to the local restaurants?

Ethan punched in some numbers, then spoke to his friend Ty. "Run this address and find out what company used this warehouse. And look for backers for the company, anything that might tell us about their trucks and shipping procedures."

She fidgeted as she waited on Ethan to finish the call.

"I want Dana to run a check on every truck the company owns," Ethan said. "Find out where they are, if they were sold to other companies, if the Sullivans might be connected to the business."

Her pulse clamored as she realized he might have a lead. Her admiration for him also rose a notch and so did her trust. Ethan wouldn't give up until they found their son. She was certain of that.

She slid her hand along his arm, silently acknowledging her confidence. He pulled her up against him, into the curve of his arm and held her close while he listened to the caller on the other end of the line. Warmth speared her body, diluting the cold that had seeped through her when she'd learned her son was missing. Some of her anger toward Ethan faded, as well. She needed him now; he needed her.

With Ethan, it had been an instant attraction. A look across the room. A smile in his eyes. A touch on the hand. A whisper of his breath on her cheek. His lips finally on hers.

And she had been his.

She still was.

The realization sent her heart into a tailspin. She had tried so hard to move on. To make a new life. To forget the connection she felt with her husband. To let the small hurts and disappointments rule her decisions instead of following her heart.

But her heart lay with Ethan. Her friend. Her lover. Her husband. The father of her child.

A child who needed them both. Not some substitute like she'd thought Frank Sullivan might be.

But how could she and Ethan work things out?

Even if they did find Jesse and get him back, nothing would have changed.

A well of sadness engulfed her. They'd still face the same problems they had encountered before. Their jobs, his Eclipse work, the distance between them, not enough time...

"Let me know what you find out, Ty." Ethan disconnected the call, then ushered her toward the car. "Come on, Bec," he said. "Let's take this blood and get it tested. Maybe by then Ty will have a lead on where Finn might have gone."

"So you're going to the police now?" Rebecca asked.

"No. I have friends at a local lab I use with other missions."

There he was with his secrecy again. She didn't ask, though, simply nodded, lost in the maze of problems they faced as he drove to the nearest lab with power. She waited in the stifling hot waiting room while Ethan rushed to confer with the technicians. The second hand on the clock ticked by in slow motion as she paced the room. Ethan finally returned, a solemn expression clouding his face.

"It's Jesse's blood, isn't it?" she asked.

He nodded.

"How can you be sure?"

"I kept a copy of his labwork from when he fell ice-skating on Frog Pond and had stitches. We compared the two."

Although she'd expected the news, the realization that Finn had actually hurt Jesse gnawed at her sanity. Where was her little boy bleeding? How badly was he hurt? Were his injuries life threatening? How much time did they have?

Ethan's phone trilled, and he answered the

call, his eyebrows scrunching. "Yes, thanks, Ty. I'll check them out now."

When he disconnected, he grabbed her hand. "Apparently Finn had a bank account near here, along with a safety deposit box. Let's check it out."

Hope sprang to life. Maybe he deposited a passport or some other information about where he might go.

A passport would mean he planned to leave the country when he was done.

They had to find him first.

FINN SMILED TO HIMSELF AS HE parked at Valerie Willings's home in Cambridge. The classic style and immaculate landscaping proved she had style and money.

All thanks to him and the stock tips he'd passed onto her. Stock tips based on Ethan Matalon's companies.

He laughed as he thought of how easy it had been. Easy to make money. Easy to seduce Valerie. Easy to have her body.

A body that had given him satisfaction

when Rebecca had forced him to wait and play the nice man in a slow game of seduction.

Finn hated slow. With women, he usually took what he wanted, a direct result of having to wait so long for other pleasures in his life. Like seeing his father released and exacting his revenge.

Now tension coiled his body, and his blood pumped fiery hot through his veins with excitement.

In fact, he needed a physical release now to temper his adrenaline and help him regain control.

Valerie would provide him with that release.

He killed the engine, then rammed his hand through his hair as he walked up to her entrance and let himself in. The sweet little secretary at his construction company owed him for helping her make her small fortune, and he never let her forget it.

The scent of furniture polish and cleaner wafted from the gleaming hardwood floors and dark paneled walls. He grinned, thinking about the irony of her being a cleaning fanatic at home but a dirty girl when she climbed in bed.

He whistled when he spotted her in the kitchen wearing nothing but a tank top and short shorts that showcased her slender tanned legs. They weren't as long as Rebecca's, but they were muscular, and she liked wrapping them around him and holding on when he rode her.

At the sound of his footfalls, she spun around from the counter where she had been kneading bread dough. Such a domestic chore for a whore.

"I think you can find a better use for those hands," he murmured with a sideways grin.

She laughed, tossing her silky auburn hair over her shoulder, then wiped the flour from her hands onto a cloth. "This needs to rise for a while anyway," she said with a twinkle in her eye.

"I know something else that is already rising." He moved toward her, then grabbed her around the waist and yanked her up against him. "I brought my camcorder. Thought we'd play a few games."

Her eyebrows lifted in curiosity. "What kind of games?"

"Naughty ones," he murmured against her ear.

She pushed her hips into his aching erection, and he groaned, then tore off her clothes. Driven by need, he took her against the counter, pounding his body into hers until she cried out her release.

"That was just the beginning," he said as his own orgasm rocked through him.

Now the fun began.

He dragged her into the bedroom and tied her to the bed. Then he set up the camera to film his show.

She protested slightly, twisting and squirming as if the bondage frightened her, but her eyes glittered with arousal. Then he blindfolded her and removed his knife. The next few minutes, he toyed with her, pressing the tip to her throat, then dragging it down her breasts. His lips traced each place the knife touched, from her luscious neck to her toes. Blood dotted her belly where the knife had slipped, and she groaned, but he licked it off.

He dragged the knife across her breasts,

making tiny slices along her nipples. This time she screamed, her fear palpable, arousing his sex to an aching hardness. Emitting a low growl, he lowered his mouth and bit her nipples, sucking and biting them so hard that tears rolled down her cheeks.

"Please, stop," she pleaded. "Frank, it's too much."

"You like the pain," he growled. "Say it, Val. Say you want more."

She shook her head, but he jabbed the tip down her cheek, and she cried out. "Yes, please…please more, Frank. Harder, make me come."

Laughing, he mounted her and pounded himself inside her again, using such force that she writhed against her restraints, but he thrust inside her again until he poured his release inside her.

She sobbed and begged for him to untie her, but he shook his head, then rose above her and made her lick him clean. When she finished, he removed her blindfold and watched her eyes widen in terror as he pressed his gun to her head. The knife had been fun, but he liked to end things with a bullet, a clean shot to the head.

The bed squeaked as she twisted, but her ragged cries and pitiful pleas were futile. He could leave no witnesses behind. Besides, he needed to finish the show for Rebecca and Ethan.

If they didn't know what kind of man he was before, they'd know with dead certainty after they saw the video.

He angled his head toward the camera. "The next time it will be you, Rebecca," he whispered. "And Matalon will get to watch."

Smiling, he shoved the gun to Valerie's head and fired.

Chapter Ten

6:00 p.m.

Ethan drove like a bat out of hell toward the bank. Every minute that ticked by his anxiety mounted, the certainty that Finn was leading him on a wild-goose chase just to torment him compounding his anger. But what else could he do? He had to follow every lead, every clue. Hopefully, Finn would make a mistake. Reveal some small detail that would give away his location.

Although, due to the blackout, Boston had called out every available officer and had stationed police at the major intersections to help smooth clogged traffic, cars still jammed the streets, their drivers honking horns and growing more agitated.

How long would the city be without power? Backup generators and battery-powered computers helped some, but that power would wane soon.

And night was quickly falling, the darkness looming bleaker and more daunting with the lights still out across the city.

An image of his son bleeding, scared and locked in that dark car trunk flashed into his head, and he silently cursed.

His stomach in knots, he maneuvered his way through the throng and parked in the lot across from the bank, swiping at a bead of sweat on his neck as he and Rebecca made their way into the bank. Most of the teller stations had been closed due to computer problems with the power outage, and he was certain the vault was inaccessible for the same reason. Frustrated people needing cash barked at the ATM machine, and an angry construction worker argued with one of the tellers that he needed to get his paycheck deposited or his account would be overdrawn. The teller assured him they would accommodate his needs, but banking had virtually come to a halt.

The guard at the door eyed him warily, and Ethan wondered if he looked as haggard as he felt. He asked to speak to the manager, then explained what he needed.

Thankfully, the safety deposit boxes didn't require electronic codes but keys instead. Five minutes later, he removed a folder from the box, and discovered several more companies Finn had invested in. Beside the investment dates, Finn had noted his profit margins.

"Son of a bitch," Ethan muttered. They were all companies Ethan owned himself. So Finn had hacked into his business information and had profited financially, then used those finances to fund his revenge scheme.

"What is it?" Rebecca asked at his muttered curse.

He explained and she rubbed his arm. "He used both of us, Ethan."

Dammit. Ethan had been too busy building his business empire and running his Eclipse missions to take care of his own family at home.

Or even to realize they were in danger.

He'd left them alone, unprotected, open targets for his enemies. When this ended, the possibility of his job jeopardizing them again remained. Ethan had countless more adversaries…

The enormity of his blindness nearly made his legs buckle.

Rebecca had said that when they got Jesse back, he should get out of their lives for good, and maybe she was right. If leaving them was the only way to protect them, he'd have to have the courage to do so.

Rebecca reached inside the box and removed another envelope, this one smaller and containing pictures of Finn with another woman.

Ethan carried the photo to the manager to see if he recognized her. "No, I don't believe I've seen her before. But you might check with the tellers."

"I will." Ethan hurried to the front and asked a short dumpy woman with frosted hair, but she shook her head. He tried two more tellers, but they didn't recognize Finn or the woman.

An Asian lady in black silk at the receptionist's desk squinted at the photo. "I think she has been in here. She just opened an account."

"Do you remember her name?" Ethan asked.

"I'm sorry, sir, but I'm not allowed to dispense information to strangers."

"Listen to me," Ethan growled in her face. "We're investigating a federal kidnapping case of a five-year-old boy." He showed her the photo of Finn and the woman from the safety deposit box. "This man has the boy. And this woman may be his accomplice."

"I—"

"I can have a warrant here within an hour," Ethan said. "But the boy's life is in danger, and you have a chance to save him by cooperating."

"Please," Rebecca said softly. "He's my son. We're running out of time."

The woman tilted her head sideways, then clicked several keys on her laptop and scrolled through the lists of new accounts, checking the names.

"This is it," she said glancing up. "Her name is Valerie Willings."

"Address?"

She recited a street in Cambridge, and he thanked her, and turned to Rebecca. "Come on, let's see if Miss Willings will talk."

Time crawled by as they drove toward the Cambridge area. "What if we're wasting our time?" Rebecca asked.

"We have to check her out." He scraped a hand along his jaw where he already needed a shave. "Besides, I think Finn left those photographs for us to find. He wants us to chase him, to have to work for every clue."

"So we're running around all over town because he's set a trail for us."

"Exactly."

"What if he's leading us astray on purpose?"

Ethan gritted his teeth. "I think he wants us to find him. He won't walk away until we meet face-to-face."

Because in the end, he wanted Ethan to see his pain. For that reason alone, Finn would stick around until he decided it was time to end the game.

Ethan just prayed that game didn't end with his son's death.

REBECCA STRUGGLED TO HANG ON TO hope as Ethan maneuvered the traffic toward Cambridge. But every second that passed, she felt her hope dwindling and her son slipping further away.

As she stared at the darkening sky, she wondered how anyone could be so cruel to a five-year-old boy.

She should have done more to protect Jesse. Maybe if she had stayed with Ethan…

Her own past flashed back. She and her father hadn't been close. In fact, he had always been walking out the door to some new company he'd funded, leaving her and her mother alone.

Then one day he'd walked out and had never come back.

In retrospect, her childhood had obviously played into her decision to leave Ethan and take the job in L.A. She'd seen herself repeating her mother's cycle. Taking a backseat to her husband's career, raising a child who constantly begged for his absentee father, waiting on the total love and devotion that would never come.

Her mother had fallen apart when her father left, leaving her even more alone. Then her mother had drifted into depression and alcohol and had never recovered. She'd died in Rebecca's teens.

At least Rebecca hadn't fallen into depression and ignored Jesse.

But she had been so lonely that she'd turned within herself and focused on her goals just like she had in high school. Back then she'd plunged into the yearbook staff full force, along with the school newspaper, and had discovered her love of reporting. In college, she'd also worked on the school newspaper, then interned at a local TV station.

She'd been on target goal-wise until she'd met Ethan and fallen hard.

They'd had a whirlwind romance filled with the best sex of her life—and so many tender moments that she still woke up in a sweat remembering them at night.

The day Jesse was born flashed back.

Ethan had been away on business. He'd never stopped working, pushing, expanding his company—and racking up profits.

That night, he hadn't been reachable when she'd gone into labor. She'd suffered back pains all night. And when she'd finally arrived at the hospital, she'd been terrified that something was wrong with the baby.

She'd been livid with Ethan, afraid he wouldn't make it there in time for the delivery.

But somehow he'd found out about her labor and had rushed into the hospital room with roses in one hand and an apology in his eyes. Fifteen minutes later, she'd given birth to their son.

And Ethan had cried.

Something about seeing her big tough, impenetrable husband so touched by his infant's arrival had dissipated any anger or disappointment she'd harbored. All that mattered was that moment, that second when she'd looked into his eyes and they had connected, had bonded with their son.

He'd refused to leave them alone that night and had slept in the chair beside her bed. In the early morning hours, she'd begged him to lie by her side.

But as combustible as they had been together, she'd needed Ethan around more and more as Jesse grew older.

Now she looked at his strong profile. That broad forehead. Hair clipped military-style. Those strong features that personified the strength in the man, both physical and mental.

The depth of his love for his son.

For her.

Where had they gone wrong? Could their marriage possibly be pieced back together?

ETHAN VEERED DOWN A TREE-LINED street of immaculate houses in a neighborhood that indicated Valerie Willings had money.

"What does this woman do?" she asked.

"I don't know. Maybe Finn set her up. He certainly made enough damn money off me to live comfortably for the rest of his sorry life."

Rebecca's stomach roiled. To think he had used Ethan's financial genius and computer know-how for his personal gain made her sick. He'd also used her—her naivete and desperation—to worm his way into her life and win her trust.

Ethan spun into the cobblestone driveway and parked, then turned to her. "You want to wait here?"

"No." She squared her shoulders. "This is my battle, too. I'm not afraid to confront Frank."

He lifted his other hand and stroked her cheek. "He's not Frank, Rebecca. That was all an act. Finn Shea has no heart or feelings for you or Jesse."

His words drove the pain and humiliation deeper. "I'm sorry if that hurts, Bec. I know you were in love with him or you wouldn't have slept with him."

Ethan looked so vulnerable that she had to be honest. Even if it meant she was a fool again.

"I wasn't in love with him, Ethan, and I never…never slept with him. I've never felt the same way about any man as I have you."

His eyes darkened, locked with hers. "Bec…"

"Shh." She reached up and kissed him

gently. "I know it's been two years and that you probably can't say the same."

He glanced down at their joined hands, and a muscle ticked in his jaw. "You may find this hard to believe, Rebecca, but I haven't been with anyone, either."

Her mouth parted in surprise while her heart somersaulted in her chest. Ethan had been celibate?

Strong, virile, sexual, animal-in-bed Ethan. A man who liked a woman's touch.

"Ethan…"

He leaned forward and claimed a kiss to her mouth. The moment was tender, erotic, full of desperate hope and passion. She wanted so much more.

But now was not the time.

Besides, she couldn't trust her feelings. Not when she was on an emotional roller coaster because of their missing son.

Nothing mattered now except finding Jesse.

As if he read her mind, he slowly pulled away. "Let's talk to Valerie Willings. Maybe she'll lead us to our little boy."

She nodded and squeezed his hand again,

then they walked up the sidewalk side by side. Her gaze sliced through the surroundings of the English Tudor house as she studied the property. Was Finn here now? Did he have cameras on his girlfriend's property? Was he watching them, laughing as they chased their tails?

Ethan pounded on the door, but no one answered, so he tried the doorknob. To her surprise, the door creaked open.

Ethan gave her a sharp look, then pushed her behind him. She communicated a silent look of understanding but followed him inside.

Eclectic artwork hung on the pale yellow walls of the foyer, while expensive leather furniture dominated the living area ahead. She inhaled furniture polish and cleaning supplies, then a sickening odor that smelled like death.

Ethan moved slowly, inching his way through the open floor plan, checking the den and kitchen. A bowl containing homemade bread dough sat on the counter, a half glass of red wine beside it, the sound of the ceiling fan in the adjoining room whirring in the silence.

"Something doesn't feel right," Ethan whispered roughly.

She nodded against his back. "You think he's here?"

"No, but he has been."

She suddenly halted, and realized he was right. The odor of Frank Sullivan's cologne permeated the room, along with the scent of sex. A pair of short shorts, a tank top and lacy black bikini panties lay in a pile on the floor by the kitchen bar.

Ethan motioned toward the hallway leading to the master suite, and she tiptoed behind him as they inched toward the room. In the background, the sound of a Barry Manilow tune wafted in the silence along with the staticky sound of a TV set.

She clutched Ethan's shoulder as they rounded the corner and peered into the ice-blue room. Inside, on a four-poster bed draped with white linens lay a woman tied spread-eagle to the bedposts.

Rebecca pressed her hand over her mouth to stifle a scream when she spotted the puddle of blood and brain matter that darkened the pillow and sheets below the woman's head.

"Dammit, we're too late again." Ethan grabbed her arms and started to push her from the room.

But she spotted the video recorder on its stand, and the television in front of the bed where a note had been taped.

"Look, Ethan."

His dark eyes cut toward the television. Recognition dawned, and he vaulted toward the TV, ripped off the note and read it.

Play me.

Ethan muttered another curse and jabbed the play button. Bile rose in Rebecca's stomach as they watched Finn tie the woman to the bedposts, tease her with the knife, then have sex with her.

Rebecca squeezed her hands into fists, knowing what was coming as the woman screamed and writhed beneath Finn. She tried to prepare herself for the ending, told herself to look away, but she couldn't tear her eyes from the screen as Finn raised the pistol and fired a bullet into Valerie Willings's head.

And when he turned toward the camera and murmured that she would be next and that Ethan would watch, a chill slid down her spine, and her legs gave way beneath her.

Chapter Eleven

Fury surged through Ethan as he stared at the TV screen. He barely resisted the urge to slam his fists into the set and break the damn thing.

What he wanted to do was break Finn Shea's face.

But he could not destroy evidence. Because when this was over, if he didn't kill Finn, which he probably would, he wanted every scrap of evidence possible to lock the man in prison for the rest of his life.

He heard Rebecca's soft wail of horror and spun around and grabbed her before her knees hit the floor.

"I can't believe that horrible man is the same Frank Sullivan who coached Jesse's team," she bit out. She clung to him and pulled herself upright. "And that he has Jesse. God, Ethan…"

He was shaking all over, too, but had to rein in his own panic. "I know, but Jesse's still alive, Bec. I feel it."

Her terrified gaze met his and she nodded, although her body jerked uncontrollably. Like him, she was unable to accept any another ending to this nightmare.

"You're right," she said, blowing out a breath. "He wants us there, wants to torture us, so he will keep him alive."

Hearing her say those words with such conviction meant more to him than he'd ever imagined. He needed her strength, her faith right now, as much as he needed his next breath.

"He led us here for a reason," Ethan said, thinking out loud. "Not just to see the tape, but to give us another clue."

Determination straightened her shoulders, and she narrowed her eyes and pulled away from his embrace to search the room. "He didn't give any hints in the video."

"No, but he killed Valerie Willings to shock us."

"And because she could recognize him," Rebecca said flatly.

He nodded. Never leave a witness behind.

He clutched her hands when she started toward the desk in the corner. "Don't touch anything. Let me get some gloves from the car. I'll be right back."

He went to his car, grabbed some plastic gloves, then punched in Dana Whitley's number as he hurried back inside to search the house. "Dana, run a check on a woman named Valerie Willings." He recited her address. "I want everything you can find on her ASAP."

Phone in hand while he waited for her response, he scrounged through the desk, where he found loose stationery with a cat border, gem clips and a day planner and checkbook. He quickly flipped through the day planner, searching the pages for information. Up until six months ago, the notations described a pretty bland life. A lunch date with a coworker at a small construction company. Dinner with a woman named Leslie. A movie date.

But six months ago, the company Valerie worked for had been bought out.

The hair on the back of his neck stood on end. Frank Sullivan had bought the company.

After that, her private life had picked up. Dates with hair stylists, manicurists, a local spa and several outings with Frank Sullivan. According to her checkbook, her income had increased drastically during that time period.

Had Finn given her a hefty raise when he'd assumed control, or had he paid her for her bedroom services?

"Ethan," Dana said. "I found a few things on her that you might be interested in. Valerie Willings works for Sullivan Construction, and owns a small portion of stock in three of your companies."

Son of a bitch. Finn had given her stock tips, and just like Finn, she had profited from Ethan's own business.

"Does she have any additional property? A second home anywhere?"

A tense moment passed. "No, but Sullivan Construction is in the middle of building a new condo development on Salem Street there in Boston."

Ethan's hand tightened around the handset. A new construction development. Empty condos, noisy workers and machinery that could drown out a child's cry.

A perfect place to hide a kidnapped victim.

REBECCA GLANCED AT HER WATCH. Six-twenty.

Over four hours since Jesse had last been seen.

Ethan massaged the tight knot at the base of her neck. "Let's check out those condos, Rebecca."

Valerie's shocked, ghostlike eyes haunted her as she gripped his hand and they walked to the car, resolute but determined, alone in their thoughts and misery but united in their mission.

For now, they were a family.

Why had it taken a traumatic situation to bring them together? Would they stay united when they rescued Jesse?

Ethan drove past the neatly lined homes in Cambridge and maneuvered the car toward Salem Street.

Rebecca's cell phone rang, jarring her. She checked the number, hoping, praying the caller was Finn. But her work number appeared on the display.

"It's the TV station," she told Ethan.

"Go ahead and answer it," he said. "But don't tell them about Jesse."

She nodded and connected the call. "Rebecca Matalon speaking."

"Rebecca, this is Judy Hatchins."

Judy, a gorgeous brunette in her thirties, was one of the news anchors at the station. Rebecca had had lunch with her a few times, considered her a friend, although Judy liked to gossip. And she had the hots for Wade Waterston, one of the investigative reporters and the most ambitious journalist at the station.

"We just received word about your son's kidnapping," Judy said, out of breath. "Good heavens, Rebecca, are you all right? Have you found Jesse? Do you know who the kidnapper is? Why he took him?"

A cold chill washed over Rebecca. "Judy, no one is supposed to know he's missing. How did you find out?"

"So it is true? Oh, my goodness…" Judy shouted. "Rebecca, we're on it now. Wade Waterston got an anonymous tip from some woman at a taxi service in Boston, said she'd recognized you when you and some guy who looked like a cop bulldozed in asking questions."

Panic clawed at Rebecca. If Judy knew, that meant the entire staff probably knew, which meant the station had the story ready to air. They wanted confirmation, and she had just given it to them.

Heaven help them. What had she done?

Ethan must have recognized the problem, because his brown eyes turned black. "What's going on?" he muttered.

She covered the mouthpiece with her hand and whispered, "Someone called in a tip about Jesse to the station. Ethan, everyone there probably knows he's been abducted by now. If the news spreads across the wire taps, then it could go nationwide."

Ethan jerked the phone from her hand. "This is Ethan Matalon, Jesse's father. Whom am I speaking with?"

"Judy Hatchins, one of the TV anchors. I'm a friend of Rebecca's and so sorry to hear about Jesse, but we'll set up a tip line right away. Is the FBI working with you?"

"No, and you'd better not air anything about my son being missing," Ethan snarled. "His life depends on it, Miss Hatchins."

"Oh, dear, I'm sorry, I'll see what I can do."

"Don't just see," Ethan snapped. "Get me the station manager *now*."

His hand trembled as he steered the car onto Salem Street.

Rebecca reached for the phone. "Let me talk to him, Ethan."

He shook his head, a muscle ticking in his jaw. A tense second later, Angus Kilpatrick must have taken the call.

Ethan abruptly explained the situation to Angus. "Not only is my son's life in jeopardy, but there's more at stake, so make sure you keep a lid on the kidnapping. If anything happens to my son because of your story-chasing, backstabbing reporters, then I'll hold you personally responsible."

Rebecca crossed her arms, angry at Ethan's

high-handedness as he disconnected the call. He'd usurped her authority with her boss. He'd exerted his control instead of trusting her to handle the situation. And he'd insulted the very core and ethics of her profession.

He cut his eyes toward her, fury blazing in their depths, along with a deep-seated panic that terrified her even more. She detested the fact that Ethan had taken charge and dismissed her.

But he was worried about his son, and he knew Finn Shea. She'd hold her tongue until they had Jesse back and Finn in custody, but then she'd confront his trust issue.

Then Wade Waterston's face flashed in her mind, and her stomach tensed. Wade would do anything to scoop another reporter and make a name for himself.

What if he didn't listen to Angus and aired the story anyway? If Finn saw it, he might get volatile and kill Jesse.

ETHAN GLARED AT THE TRAFFIC, wondering why the hell people couldn't stay at home when they were in the middle of a damn blackout? Anger and fear seized his nerve endings as he contemplated the fact that the people at Rebecca's station had found out about Jesse's kidnapping. An "anonymous tip"? What was she—some do-gooder or someone wanting money for information?

Damn vulture reporters. They didn't care about justice or helping the law, only seeing their names in the paper or their faces on camera. They'd sensationalize their own mother's death just to get attention.

He glanced at Rebecca and noted the tense way she'd squared her shoulders. She'd folded her arms and had turned to stare out the window, the strain evident on her pale face. He wanted to comfort her, and whisper promises, but if her people didn't listen to his orders, they could cause his son's death.

And he couldn't bear that loss.

He spotted the condo development under construction and scanned the area for trucks, for onlookers…for Finn.

The skyscraper development was partially complete, various buildings in different stages of construction, although the blackout would no doubt throw them off schedule. The west-side buildings appeared to be almost complete but unoccupied, while the east side was clearly in the early stages with only the foundation.

He angled his head to search for signs of life, but spotted nothing. Was Jesse being held inside one of the dark buildings?

Rebecca's sigh dragged him back to her. "What do we do now?" she asked quietly.

"I'm going to check out the condos."

"I'll go with you."

They emerged from the car quickly, and Ethan grabbed a couple of flashlights from the trunk. Although there were only two floors of the complex completed, the task seemed daunting as they climbed through the rubble of turned dirt and stone and made their way up to the west side. The next half hour dragged by as they searched each condo. One by one they eliminated the first floor. By the time they reached the second, the hair on the back of Ethan's neck prickled. He surveyed the area, then glanced down to see if Finn was hiding in the shadows watching. Laughing. Enjoying making them chase their tails.

"Dammit, I don't think he's here," Ethan said.

Rebecca gave him a helpless look, her eyes haunted. "We can't give up, Ethan. We have to search."

He nodded, and walked to the entrance to the first condo, but suddenly the hair on his neck stood on end again. Just as he always sensed trouble before a mission, he sensed it now. The air felt different. Smelled different. A zing went up his spine.

A trap.

Finn had been here, and set them up.

He hesitated before reaching for the doorknob, then pushed open the door to the unfinished room inside. The squeak of the door ended with a thundering boom. Rebecca screamed, and he grabbed her and yanked her sideways to avoid the worst of the explosion.

The walls and floor shook, glass shattered and pelted them, then the sound of falling rock and gravel echoed. The building was going down.

Cold terror washed over him.

Was this the way it would end?

Had Finn brought them here so he could kill them all together?

REBECCA DUCKED HER HEAD AS Ethan threw his arms over her to protect her from flying debris. All around her, the building trembled, plaster rained down and the walls crumbled. Fire exploded in patches inside the condo and shattered glass sprayed them.

Ethan clutched her tightly, his breathing as erratic as her own heart pounding in her chest. When the first wave settled, he tested the flooring, and they both pivoted on their bellies to study the remaining structure.

"Bec, are you hurt?"

Her knees stung and so did her hands, but thanks to him, she had escaped any serious injuries. "I'm all right. Are you?"

"Fine."

"What if Jesse was in there?"

"I'll find out."

He pushed up onto his knees, and she did the

same, ready to follow him, but he folded her hands in his. "Stay here. It's too dangerous."

Fear darkened his eyes, then he turned and ran into the blazing condo, yelling Jesse's name. Rebecca's heart clenched. Ethan would do anything for his son.

She couldn't lose him or Jesse.

Heat seared her as she darted into the condo behind him and screamed Jesse's name. Orange and yellow flames clawed at the walls and smoke filled her nostrils. She covered her mouth but forged forward. Ethan ran into one bedroom and she took the other, her pulse clamoring when she spotted a pile of debris near what would have been the door to a closet.

She jumped over a patch of flames and dug her way through the mess, tossing splintered wood and pieces of concrete to the side.

Her breath caught as she spotted the brim of a cap beneath the mess. She dug it out and screamed in horror.

It was Jesse's Red Sox cap.

Behind the cap, the rest of the closet burst into flames.

Ethan ran inside and grabbed her. "Rebecca—"

Her hand shook violently as she lifted the cap. "It's Jesse's."

Ethan's jaw tightened in pain, then his gaze swung toward the burning closet, and he howled like a wild animal.

A second later, a siren wailed and firemen suddenly burst onto the scene, grabbing them and forcing them outside. She clung to Ethan who moved on autopilot, both numb and silent as they clutched their son's hat between them.

"Check the closet, see if there's a body…" Ethan mumbled to the fireman. "A child… got to find him."

"You think someone was in there?" the man asked.

"Just check, dammit." Ethan held up the cap. "This was my son's. It was near the door."

Sympathy registered in the man's eyes, then he nodded, turned and ran back up the steps, barking commands to his team that a child might possibly be inside, to search for a body.

Rebecca shivered. No… It was impossible. Jesse couldn't be dead. Not this way. Not in a fire…

A sob caught in her throat, then she dragged in a breath, and felt herself falling to her knees. Ethan caught her just as her cell phone rang.

Her heart racing, she fumbled inside her purse. The display box showed an out of area signal, but Rebecca knew who it was before she pressed the connect button. Ethan obviously did, too, and grabbed the phone from her.

"You bastard—"

"I warned you not to call the police or tell anyone." Finn's deep voice echoed with menace. "Now your son's blood is on your hands, Matalon."

Chapter Twelve

Ethan had to hold it together for Rebecca's sake. She needed him to be strong. To offer hope.

But inside he was dying.

Rage fueled his temper and gave him strength as he imagined finding Finn Shea and tearing him apart limb by limb. No amount of torture would be enough to satisfy Ethan's need for revenge.

Tears burned his throat and the back of his eyelids, and his body shook with anguish. A police siren wailed in the distance, jarring him back to reality. He didn't want to deal with the cops. Couldn't. Not yet.

Not until he knew for sure that his son had been in the fire.

No…

Finn had to be lying. Taunting him. Trying to cause him pain. Dragging out his twisted game.

Ethan couldn't have lost Jesse…

Rebecca trembled, and he clutched her against him, holding on to her to keep her upright, and to keep him sane.

"Bec, the cops are coming. I'm going to talk to the fireman, then we have to get out of here."

"No. Not until we know…"

"Trust me, Bec."

"What are you going to do?"

He knew the fireman would insist they stay. He was obligated to. But Ethan couldn't talk to the police yet. "Whatever I have to."

Her pain-glazed eyes met his, and his heart spasmed, emotions nearly choking him. Soot blackened her cheeks, dots of blood from the cuts on her hands had streaked his shirt and she had a gash on her forehead that he was certain she was unaware of.

An ambulance siren cut through the night, close behind the police's wail, and Ethan clutched her tighter. If Finn was toying with them and Jesse was still alive, they had to leave.

He coaxed Rebecca to sit down on the stoop, and he rushed up the steps and found the fireman he'd spoken to earlier. The sound of the other rescue workers yelling back and forth mingled with the angry roar of the fire and crumbling debris. Orange and red flames shot up into the sky.

Sweat streaked the man's face and uniform as he conferred with one of the men spraying water on the flames.

The fireman's expression turned grave as he faced Ethan. "We haven't found anyone yet, sir. We'll have to wait until the fire dies out and cools before we can check the ashes."

"You have to check," Ethan said. "I have to know if my son was in there."

"What were the two of you doing here?" the fireman asked.

"Our son…he got lost in the blackout. He… We were looking at buying a place here, and thought he might have wandered over."

The fireman's eyes narrowed in disbelief.

"Listen, my wife is in shock, I'm going to take her home—"

"The paramedics are on their way," the fireman said, straightening in suspicion. "And the police need your statement to investigate. You're a material witness."

Desperation made Ethan pull his weapon. "Listen to me very carefully. I'm an undercover agent working a kidnapping case. The boy was taken earlier this evening, and I can't talk to the local police here or they'll kill the boy."

"You're a federal agent?"

"Yes," Ethan lied. "I'm also the boy's father, and that's his mother. She…she's terrified right now."

"Then I'd think you'd want to stay and make sure your son isn't inside."

"I do want that, but if he's not and I talk to the cops right now, our son will be dead within the hour. The kidnapper's watching."

The man's eyes met Ethan's, searching, unconvinced. Hardening. "Put the gun away, Mister. You don't want to do this. Arson is one thing, but murder is another."

"I didn't set the fire, dammit," Ethan snarled. Desperate, he pulled out his wallet and showed the man a photo of his son. "This is my son, the boy I'm searching for. The one who might be in there." His voice cracked, his hands shook. "He's five years old. His name is Jesse. He loves the Red Sox, and hot dogs and skating on Frog Pond. I promised I'd teach him to sail one day, and he wants a dog that I never got him…. He's my only child." Ethan's voice broke with emotions. "Please, I can't lose him."

A heartbeat of silence followed. Then the sirens wailed closer and tires screeched in the parking lot.

Ethan cut his gaze toward the police car, fear grappling with panic.

He must have convinced the fireman that he was legitimate, because he gave a clipped nod. "Get going."

Ethan squeezed the man's arm. "Here's my card, and my address is on it for later. I'll make a formal statement once we find Jesse. Call me and let me know…"

He couldn't finish the sentence.

Compassion filled the man's eyes, then Ethan turned and ran back to Rebecca.

He'd take her back to his house, make sure she was safe. Get someone to stay with her if he needed.

Then he'd track down Finn Shea and kill him.

A COLD NUMBNESS SPREAD THROUGH Rebecca as Ethan drove back to his brownstone.

Images of Jesse filled her head. Jesse when he was born. A tiny seven-pound baby in her arms. The first time he'd smiled and cooed at her. The first time he'd pushed up to crawl.

His first step at nine months.

His first word. *Dada.* The way he'd smashed peas and applesauce in his baby-fine blond hair. The time he'd colored with red crayons all over the wall. The morning he'd jammed an M&M's candy up his nose and they'd rushed him to the emergency room.

The look on his face when Ethan had taken him to his first Red Sox game. Christmas when he'd laughed as they'd decorated sugar cookies and made homemade gingerbread ornaments for the tree. The surprise on his face when he'd discovered the train set Ethan had bought him when he was three. The day Ethan had taught him to swim. The day Jesse had learned to ride a bike.

The tears in his big eyes when she'd told him they were moving to L.A. without Ethan.

Emotions choked her, along with remorse for not trying harder to keep their family together. And anger at Finn Shea for robbing them of the chance to fix things now.

She glanced at Ethan and saw the anguish in his brown eyes. Tears clogged her throat, but she was too numb to speak.

He parked in his garage, came around and guided her inside his house. Darkness was falling over the interior, but he lit several candles, then led her to his bedroom.

There he lit more candles, dappling the room in a soft yellow glow. Time blurred as he guided her to the bathroom. She felt weighted, struggling with despair and desolation. Her arms felt empty.

She'd never hold her son again.

Tears suddenly spilled over, and Ethan

clutched her in his arms and held her, rocking her back and forth as she wept. She sobbed and muttered Jesse's name over and over while he soothed her with nonsensical words, his body shuddering, too, with grief.

Slowly, they moved into the bathroom, where he began to undress her. She didn't protest, only allowed him to help her step into the shower. She was vaguely aware of the blood dotting her clothes and hands, and the scent of smoke permeating her clothing.

He stripped then and climbed inside with her, turning the hot water on them both to break the chill that had invaded her. Ethan grabbed the bath sponge and soaped it, then gently washed the cut on her face, her neck, her arms, then slid it over her body. His tenderness made the tears flow again, but he didn't stop. He continued to bathe her, touching her so gently that she ached for more. For the closeness of his body against her, making her forget the pain.

He ran the soft sponge over her breasts, making them tingle, then slid it down her stomach to her thighs, turned her around and started on her back, over her shoulders, down the curve of her spine, over her hips and buttocks. She closed her eyes, willing the pain to ease as his hand moved between her legs and he bathed her essence.

Finally she turned back to him, looked into his eyes, saw the same grief she felt mirrored in the tears glistening in his brown eyes. The depth of his own pain sent a spasm of heartache through her, yet for a moment, she forgot her own pain in the wake of wanting to ease his.

She pressed a hand to his cheek and held it while their gazes locked. Without speaking, she took the sponge from him, soaped it again and dragged it over his shoulders. He winced as if hurting, and she knew that he felt suddenly vulnerable, afraid to show his grief to her.

He was so strong, tough, so much the man she had fallen in love with.

If ever he needed her, he needed her now. Just as she needed him.

She bathed his chest, watching quietly as the soap bubbles dotted the dark hair, her pulse clamoring as his heartbeat pulsed beneath her hand. She dragged the sponge lower, washed his flat washboard belly. His sex hardened and jutted forward.

Instead of touching him, though, she turned him around as he had her, and gently soaped the broad expanse of his back and wide shoulders, then lower to his firm buttocks. Dropping to her knees, she soaped his hairy legs, muscular calves, then coached him to pivot and bathed his sex.

He groaned and threw his head back, then reached down and dragged her upright in front of him. His eyes flared with need, hunger, a burning desire to have her that caused heat to shoot through her. Her nipples stiffened, liquid warmth pooled between her thighs. As if he sensed the tension coiling inside her, he lowered his head and flicked his tongue along the turgid peak.

She shivered, and clutched his arms, hating that she needed him so, that Ethan was the only man who'd ever made her so wanton with desire that she'd begged.

But she did now.

"Please, Ethan."

"Please, what?"

"Please, make love to me."

He groaned, then captured her nipple in his mouth and sucked hard, drawing a cry of pure pleasure from her as he slid his fingers between her thighs and sank them inside her.

ETHAN HAD ONLY MEANT to comfort Rebecca. She'd been in shock, cold with pain and grief, and he'd worried she needed medical attention.

So he'd done the only thing he knew to warm her and comfort her. He'd taken her into his arms and got her warm in the shower.

He'd never meant for it to go this far.

But one touch of her skin, and need consumed him. Bathing her had stirred his sex and passion, but he'd forced himself to tamp down his desire.

Then she'd touched him.

Sorrow, fear and rage fired his hunger to a fever pitch, and he suckled her harder, driving his fingers deep inside her to find her warmth, to feel her soft feminine body clench with the need to have him fill her. He consoled himself with the sweet sound of her moans while he prayed one momentary reprieve from his search would not cost them, but would renew their energy.

"Ethan, please, I need you."

"I need you, too, Bec." Standing, he slid his hands beneath her hips and picked her up, bringing her body down onto his shaft. He plastered them against the wall of the shower, jerked his hips upward and thrust inside her, grinding their bodies together.

She cried his name, clutched his arms and kissed him, delving her tongue in his mouth as he pumped harder and faster into her. Skin slapped against skin, tongues danced and mated, and her nipples scraped his bare chest until he throbbed with the need for release.

But he had to pleasure her first.

Starving for the sound of her pleasure, he dragged his mouth from hers, bit her neck, then lowered his head and suckled her breasts again, thrusting ever deeper inside her. "Give yourself to me, Becca," he whispered hoarsely. "Let it go, let me have you."

She sobbed his name, then dropped her head against him, and nibbled at his neck.

He braced their bodies with one hand against the wall, then cupped her hand into his other.

"I love you, Bec. I've never stopped loving you."

Tears sparkled in her eyes, then she threw her head back and clawed his arms as her body spasmed around him.

REBECCA FELL AGAINST ETHAN, quivering with the aftermath of her climax. The need and hunger that had driven them together still simmered inside her, yet the reality of their son's possible death speared her with such grief that emotions overcame her, and she simply buried her head in his neck, limp and helpless.

Ethan murmured her name, then reached around her and turned off the water, which had grown cold. With one hand, he grabbed one of his oversize plush towels and wrapped it around her, then stood her on her feet and dried her. A shudder rippled through her, and his gaze met hers, then he helped her into the terry-cloth robe he kept on the door. The one that had once belonged to her.

He hadn't gotten rid of it in the two years they'd been apart, just as he hadn't removed his wedding band. And he'd said he loved her when he was inside her.

But what would happen now?

If Jesse was…gone, how could they possibly make their marriage work? The heartache and grief, the shared memories, the guilt…

Would they ever be able to overcome it?

Chapter Thirteen

7:30 p.m.

Rebecca was shutting down. Ethan felt her withdrawal as clearly as he felt the grief and fear clawing at him.

Their despair had brought them together.

Would it also tear them apart?

He scooped her up into his arms and carried her toward the bed. The day's trauma had taken its toll and she needed rest. Although he knew neither of them could really sleep or rest until they knew Jesse was safe.

"Bec, talk to me, sweetheart." He settled her on the bed and wrapped the sheet and blanket around her, then lay down beside her and cradled her in his arms. She rolled sideways, putting her back to him, but he was determined that she not shut him out, so he spooned her, wrapping his arms and legs around her so that their bodies melded together almost as one.

She sighed softly, accepting his comfort, and he breathed in the sweet scent of the soap on her skin and the fragrance of her unique body, so tempting, so tantalizing, so damn good. He wanted her again.

But not now. They had to rest for a moment, regroup, then he had to get back to work.

She nuzzled closer to him but remained quiet. For some reason the silence that lingered between them was far worse than an outburst.

He gently stroked her hair away from her cheek. "Please talk to me, Bec. Cry, scream at me, hit me if you need to. I know if we lose our son that it's all my fault."

She made a low throaty sound that pinched at his gut.

"When you first left for L.A., I told myself that we'd work things out," he said gruffly. "I was so wrapped up in my company, my financial portfolio…and still trying to save the world."

"Ethan—"

"No, let me finish," he said. "I was a coward, Bec. My dad died when I was little. He got killed overseas on an army mission. I guess I thought I was supposed to be like him."

Rebecca traced a finger over his hand. "He died a hero. I can understand you wanting to follow in his footsteps."

"But he left me," he said quietly. "After that I tried not to love anyone too much again."

His admission tore open the wall holding back his emotions, and he shuddered against her. "And now look what I've done. I've failed you both."

Rebecca turned toward him then. He didn't release her, kept her pinned in his embrace. He needed her warmth, her body next to his. He knew he was being selfish, but he couldn't lose her now or he'd die, too.

She slowly lifted her hand and splayed her fingers along his cheek. "Ethan, this is not your fault. It's that madman Finn Shea's."

"No, Bec, it *is* my fault. I was supposed to

take care of you, to protect my family, my child." Disgust and self condemnation laced his voice. "What kind of man am I to—"

"Listen to me, Ethan Matalon, you are not to blame. You love Jesse and he knows it. And I trust that you'll find him, that is if…"

Her voice broke and she couldn't continue the sentence.

"Bec…"

"What's wrong with me, Ethan?" Rebecca suddenly cried. "They say that mothers have a connection with their children. So why don't I know for sure if Jesse is alive or if he died in that fire?" She stroked his chest. "Shouldn't I be able to feel whether he's still with us?"

Ethan's heart squeezed. He understood her silence now and was glad she'd finally opened up. He felt raw, exposed, but he didn't care. Jesse was far too important to worry about pride. And so was Rebecca.

He had to fight for them both. He had to get Jesse back.

Even if Rebecca walked away from him in the end.

REBECCA BURIED HER FACE against Ethan's warm chest, craving his touch and comforting voice. She had never felt so desolate and terrified in her life.

If Jesse had been in that explosion…

No, she couldn't believe it. She wouldn't be able to go on.

"You are a wonderful mother," Ethan said softly. "That's one of the things I love about you."

Rebecca sighed and hugged him tighter.

"Sometimes at night this past year," he continued, "as I lay in bed, I'd see your face in my mind. I'd remember the first time I kissed you. The night I proposed. And the image of you holding our son when he was born will forever be etched in my mind." Emotions thickened his voice, and he rubbed his fingers down her arm. "I've never seen anything so beautiful as that sight."

"Beautiful?" Rebecca laughed softly. "You were delusional, Ethan. I was sweating and swollen and my hair was a mess."

"That's because you'd been fighting to bring our little boy into the world. And he was stubborn and took a long time, and I wasn't around to help you."

"You made it in time," Rebecca whispered. "And he was worth every moment. Every labor pain and muscle ache."

He nuzzled her neck. "I know. I saw in your eyes how much you loved him, and that made me love you even more. There was a sweet motherly instinct combined with a fierce protective look on your face that told me your bond with Jesse would never be broken."

"I did feel that way," she whispered against his arm. "So excited and so nervous at the same time. I was overwhelmed with feelings and terrified that this tiny life was completely dependent on us."

"I felt the same way."

Rebecca threaded her fingers through his. "Remember the day we brought him home? I was so nervous, afraid I'd do something wrong, that I'd drop him or wouldn't have enough milk to satisfy him."

He squeezed her breasts. "He was a pig, ate all the time."

"And I kept checking his breathing every few minutes, just to make sure he was okay."

"I used to do the same thing," Ethan admitted, pulling her closer.

"I never knew that."

He pressed a kiss to her forehead and shrugged. "I kept thinking I was in a dream, and that one day I'd wake up and you would both be gone, just like my father."

"Where did we go wrong, Ethan?"

He gritted his jaw. "I wasn't there," he said simply. "I...don't know why... Maybe I was more afraid than I realized, so I sabotaged our marriage without even realizing it."

She cradled his face in her hands. "Our baby...he can't be gone, Ethan. He just can't be... He's my whole life."

He tightened his grip on her. "We will find him, Bec. In fact, I've been thinking about that call from Finn, wondering how he knew about the TV station."

Rebecca frowned. "I don't know."

"Your phone," Ethan said, tensing. "Finn must have bugged it."

Rebecca gasped. "He was listening when Judy called me."

Ethan tucked an errant strand of her silky blond hair behind her ear, his own eyes registering the same dark terror and rage that she felt.

His cell phone rang, cutting through the tension, and he jerked upright and grabbed it. "Ethan Matalon. Yes…" He mouthed the word *fireman* to her, and her heart hammered in her chest.

This was the call they'd been waiting for—the fireman who was supposed to call if they found Jesse's body. She clasped her hands together and prayed the building had been empty.

FINN PACED THE NARROW ALLEYWAY near the condo development, a smile of satisfaction curving his mouth as he watched the orange flames shoot up into the darkening sky. The tortured look on Matalon's face when the condo had exploded had been priceless. Still, anger knotted the muscles at the back of his neck. He couldn't believe Rebecca had talked to the TV station. Hadn't he warned them?

Did they think he was joking? That he was stupid? That he wouldn't hurt the kid?

He had a damn inclination to cut the boy into a zillion pieces and send him back to them limb by limb just to show them that he wasn't messing around.

Get control. Take a deep breath.

He couldn't go off half-cocked. His father needed him. They'd plotted this mission for too long. One mistake, and they'd all get caught. And he didn't intend to end up locked in a cage like his dad had for years. He'd go crazy as hell.

No, he had to act rationally. Follow the plan.

Besides, just for a fraction of a second, he'd looked into the kid's eyes and questioned whether or not he really could kill him in the end.

For just a moment, he'd seen a scared little boy. A boy like he'd been when his father had been ripped from his life.

A boy like he might have some day.

As much as it pained him to admit it, when

he'd coached those damn kids, they'd gotten to him. Made him think that when this was over, he might settle down, find him a wife and have a rugrat himself. Provided it was a boy, of course. No whiny good-for-nothing girls.

Jesus, what was he thinking? He couldn't go soft now. They were too close to the big showdown.

He wiped at the sweat soaking his hair, smelling gasoline and smoke.

He craved the smell of blood. Matalon's.

He glanced at his watch, then phoned his father to check in.

"Finn, how's it going on that end?" Liam asked.

Finn chuckled, then explained about the fire.

"I wish I could have been there and seen Matalon's face," Liam said.

"It was perfect," Finn said. "But we may have a problem. Rebecca talked to someone from the TV station in L.A."

His father released a string of expletives. "Are they going public?"

"Matalon jumped on the line and ordered them not to," Finn said. "He threatened to sue the station if they did. I think he convinced them to hold off."

"Well, it'll all come out eventually," Liam said. "But Davis has to pay first."

"How's your situation?" Finn asked.

"Everything's in place. In fact, it's time for you to finish up with Matalon. I may need you for the next phase of the mission."

Finn twisted his lips into a grin. "Great. I'll make the call to Matalon. I'll let you know when the job is finished."

"Good. And, Finn," Liam said. "Don't forget. We don't want any witnesses left behind."

"Got it." Finn hung up and walked toward the truck he'd driven to the condo development. Time to snatch the kid and end the fun.

Excitement zinged through him. The best part was yet to come.

Chapter Fourteen

Ethan gripped the phone in a white-knuckled grip as he waited for the fire-man's report.

"We found bones," the man said.

The breath he'd been holding gushed from Ethan's chest. "Oh, God…"

"They're small," the man continued, "but I think they may belong to an animal."

Relief surged through Ethan. "Then my son wasn't in the fire?"

Rebecca made a low, whimpery sound in her throat, her body coiled tight with anxiety.

Tension held Ethan immobile. From the man's hesitation, he sensed that he wasn't finished with his report, that bad news might follow.

The fireman cleared his throat. "I'm afraid I can't completely rule out the possibility until we examine the ashes, sir."

He gritted his teeth to keep from shouting an obscenity. "I understand." Although he wanted conclusive results, he had to latch on to the thread of hope they'd been given. "Let me know what you find out."

"Any word on your boy?" the man asked gruffly.

Ethan slid his arm around Rebecca and cradled her closer. "No, not yet."

A long hesitation, then Ethan thanked him and hung up.

Rebecca clutched his hand between both of hers. "He wasn't in there, was he? Please tell me they didn't find Jesse's body."

"No, they didn't find him," Ethan said, his voice cracking.

"That's good, right?"

The desperate need to believe flared in her eyes, and he couldn't bear to break the tentative hope she was hanging on to.

"Yes." He stood and grabbed his boxers. "I have to get back to work and find him."

Rebecca nodded. "What do we do now?"

"Why don't you grab a quick shower? I'm going to call Ty. See what else he might have found out about Shea."

She slipped from the bed, naked and gorgeous, those mile-long killer legs of hers eliciting another wicked response from his body. He wanted to be back in bed with her with those legs wrapped around him. He wanted to be back inside her, filling her, hearing her cry his name as he pleasured her. Having her alleviate the fear that still pressed relentlessly against his chest.

He wanted his son back, and he wanted Finn Shea to suffer the way he and Rebecca had suffered the past few hours.

The need for revenge ate at him, making him realize how strongly Finn's own hatred and anger ran.

He spotted Jesse's Red Sox cap, picked it up and squeezed it in his hands. "Hang in there, Jesse. Just a little while longer, and I'll find you, son." Then he'd bring him home and never let him out of his sight again.

JESSE WAS TRYING TO BE BRAVE. But he was hot and tired, and he wanted his mommy and daddy.

His stomach growled, reminding him that he'd been there a long time. Was his mommy fixing dinner now?

No, they were in Boston. They'd be going out to eat. He was supposed to see his daddy tonight.

Jesse tried to think about his father and be brave like him. He missed him so much since they'd moved to L.A. But his daddy was so busy and sometimes he forgot to come and get Jesse. Would he forget tonight? Did he even know Mr. Frank had taken him?

He shivered in spite of being so hot inside the truck. Yes, his mommy must know by now. And she'd call his father. His daddy was an important man. And he was big. He'd fight mean Mr. Frank and then they'd go to a ballgame together.

He closed his eyes and tried to see the stadium in his mind. He could hear the fans cheering. See the players running on the field. Hear the announcer.

He and his father would eat hot dogs with mustard and ketchup, and his daddy would let him sip a soda, and maybe even buy him candy. And when they were leaving with the crowd, he'd ride him on his shoulders so he wouldn't get lost in the crowd.

Jesse tried to swallow, but his throat was so dry and scratchy from yelling for help that it hurt. He wanted a soda now. At least some water.

But mean Mr. Frank had left him here and hadn't come back. How long had it been? Hours? A day?

More tears pushed at the back of his eyelids, but he blinked them back in the darkness. He was getting used to it now, but he still hated it. Sometimes when he blinked he saw monsters in the shadows.

His hand tightened around the neon wand, and he thought about flipping it back on. But he made himself wait. Flashlights ran on batteries, and sometimes those gave out. The wand might give out, too.

And he didn't want the light to burn out before Mr. Frank came back.

Because when Mr. Frank opened the door, Jesse would run. Then he'd need the light to show him the way back to his parents.

He was trying to be brave, but his heart pounded with fear. He wished he knew where he was. Even if he got away, where would he run?

One thing at a time, he told himself. First, run from Mr. Frank. Then he'd figure out the rest. He was only five but he was smart for five. His mommy always said so. And so did his daddy.

He pictured his parents' faces in his mind, and his chin wobbled. Were they hunting for him? Would they find him before Mr. Frank came back?

A noise sounded outside, and footsteps clattered on the pavement. Then something hit the side of the truck, making it vibrate. It sounded like a fist.

The truck door banged shut, and the engine rumbled. Suddenly, the truck was moving, bouncing over ruts in the road. It swerved sideways, and Jesse tried to grab something to hold on to, but his hand hit air, and he rolled to the far side of the truck. His head banged the cold metal, and the black darkness spun around him as the truck sped up.

Sweat rolled down his forehead into his eyes. Mr. Frank had come back, but he hadn't opened the door, so Jesse couldn't escape.

Where was he taking him now? Back to his daddy, or someplace where his daddy couldn't find him?

ETHAN TRACED A FINGER OVER THE photograph he kept of Jesse in his wallet, swallowing his fear as he explained to Ty about the explosion at the condominium development.

"Sounds like Shea, all right." Ty's voice reeked with strain. "I hope you find Jesse, Ethan. And I hope you and Rebecca work things out. You two belong together. Something good should come out of this horrible event."

Tension drew Ethan's shoulders upward. He wanted them together, but if they didn't find Jesse, how would Rebecca ever forgive him?

"Did you find out anything else about Finn? Some place he might have taken Jesse?"

Ty sighed. "No, I've been busy following

leads on the vice-president and how Liam set up this blackout. I have a bad feeling, Matalon, that there's a bigger agenda here."

"Even bigger than getting back at Davis?"

"Yes. Or maybe it's just how he plans to get back at Davis. Liam doesn't seem to mind who or how many he hurts."

"True. The blackout has already impacted Boston's economy and created crime and chaos in the town."

Ethan scrubbed a hand over his bleary eyes. "Are you thinking a possible terrorist attack?"

The tense silence that followed vibrated with the truth, that a terrorist act was definitely worrying Ty.

"Have you alerted Homeland Security?" Ethan asked.

"Yes, and the airports are being monitored, as well."

Boston was a major port for cargo and cruise ships. In one year, the port handled over 175,000 container ships, including petroleum, liquefied natural gas, automobiles and cement. Since 9/11, the government had worried about a dirty bomb attack via the ports and had taken steps to beef up security, but in the midst of a blackout…

"Make sure to alert the State Police, Coast Guard and Massachusetts Port Authority."

"Done."

The possibility was mind-boggling. If an attack had been planned, they could attack the natural gas terminal, the Chelsea River depots, Charlestown, East Boston, South Boston, Everett…

With police already stretched to the limits because of the blackout, it would be easy to slip through the cracks.

"I'm sorry I can't help you more with Jesse," Ty said gruffly. "But we have to find the vice-president and discover what Liam has up his sleeve and stop him. The blackout can last only so long before power is restored. I have a feeling Liam is going to act in the next few hours."

"I understand," Ethan said with a knot in his throat. Liam had had plenty of time to plot his mission since he'd been released from prison. And who knew what contacts he'd made on the inside?

God, the thought was daunting.

Ty needed his help now.

But he couldn't leave Rebecca, couldn't turn his back on his own son. Besides, if he found Finn, maybe he would lead them to his father and the master plan.

"Finn and his family would know the airports are covered," Ethan said. "It also makes sense that if they're planning an escape, they might use one of the ports."

"Maybe that's where Finn has Jesse," Ty suggested.

Ethan's hands felt clammy. Maybe. But where should he look? Between the Neponset River, the Weymouth Fore River, the Weymouth Back River, the Weir River and the Atlantic, not to mention three major bays, Boston was one damn big port with waterways and ships everywhere.

Hunting one man and small boy was like finding a needle in a haystack.

"Have you sent photos of all the Sheas to the port authorities and officials?"

"Done," Ty replied.

"Let me do some more research on Finn,"

Ethan said. "Maybe I'll find something that will tell me where he is now."

Ty told him to keep in touch, then hung up. Ethan turned to his computer, frustrated but determined. He was a computer genius. There had to be some link he could find somewhere that would lead him to the man who'd kidnapped his son.

Hoping for something new, something he hadn't uncovered yet, he spent the next few minutes researching Finn—where he'd grown up, where he'd moved, anything he could find on the companies he owned or had invested in.

None of the companies that Finn had inadvertently received tips on from Ethan involved shipping, exports or imports. Finally, buried amid the information on Finn's past and his childhood with his mother, Ethan found a reference to a cottage on one of the smaller islands off Boston Harbor.

Rebecca emerged from the bedroom, dressed and smelling like fresh soap and sweet shampoo, and his body hardened. Yet he forced himself to keep working.

She inched up behind him and slid a hand to his shoulder. "Did you find anything?"

"I don't know, but there's a notation about a privately owned cottage on Peddocks Island."

"I thought most of the islands in the Boston Harbor Island National Recreational Area were uninhabited."

"True," Ethan said. "A couple house parks that are accessible by ferry, but several can be reached only by private boat."

"What about Peddocks?"

"A ferry runs seasonally. It's a long shot, but I think we should check it out. There's an old fort there, Fort Andrews, on the eastern end. It was a defense fort until the end of World War II. I heard Liam talk about it once. I think his father or grandfather was stationed there."

"So it has some meaning for Finn," Rebecca said, seeing his logic.

Ethan nodded. "Maybe he's hiding out there with Jesse."

Rebecca reached for her purse. "Then let's go check it out."

Ethan prayed they weren't chasing their tails again. But he had no other leads right now.

And after talking to Ty, if Jesse was still alive, he sensed time was running out for all of them.

REBECCA TRIED TO HOLD ON TO hope, but when they arrived at the ferry, it was closed. Despair threatened as unanswered questions engulfed her. Where was her son? Was he safe? Did he even know they were looking for him?

The images of the explosion at the condo complex flashed in her mind, but she banished them. Ethan had told her that Jesse hadn't been in there…

"I'll commandeer a boat," Ethan said as he headed over to the dock to talk to a fisherman.

She stared at the sky, into the coming blackness. Void of stars or moonlight tonight, the abyss mirrored the aching emptiness in her soul. An emptiness that could only be filled if her son was found alive.

The whisper of fear that had dogged her all day returned to chase a chill up her spine. The sound of a motorboat churning through the waves mingled with the choppy swish of water bouncing off the dock's edge, while the pungent scent of fish and oil permeated the air, reminding her of the first time she and Ethan had ridden the ferry to Long Island with Jesse. He had been so excited to stand on the seat and feel the wind in his hair, so thrilled to be going on an adventure.

She wanted to give him more adventures, more family trips.

Ethan returned and ushered her toward a small private boat, then helped her climb inside it. She clung to the sides as he switched on the motor, and the boat catapulted forward, zipping through the inlet toward the island, spraying her with water.

It seemed like hours later, but had been only minutes when they reached the small island.

"The fort is on the eastern end," Ethan said. "But it's defunct now, and the cottages are on the southern end." The reason he'd gone to the tip of the island.

He maneuvered the boat into a small cove, anchored it, then helped her out. Together they climbed the embankment and hiked across the terrain toward the cottages. The scent of the fresh water marsh filled the air, and as they hiked along the shore, Rebecca noticed wild roses growing in the distance near the row of cottages.

"Which one belongs to Finn?"

Ethan recited the address and she began to walk faster. She just hoped Jesse was inside, and that they could finally confront the man who'd stolen him from them.

But as they neared the cottage, her hopes dwindled. Shadows bathed the cottage, which appeared to be empty. The front door had been boarded up, the lot unkempt, the paint peeling, the wood rotting.

"Ethan?"

His expression registered the same disappointment she felt. "I'll check inside."

She nodded and followed him up the steps, wincing when they creaked beneath her feet. There was no evidence that anyone had been here lately. No footprints on the muddy steps, and cobwebs still stretched across the screened doorway.

She peeked through the window, but it was so black inside that nothing was visible.

Ethan walked around back, then returned a minute later. "I thought there might be a back door, but it's been boarded up, too. And it doesn't look like anyone has been here."

Still, he tore off the boards from the front door. Finn could have ripped them away, tied Jesse inside, then boarded the house back up, thinking no one would ever find him. Jesse might be inside alone. Hurt and bleeding. Cold and scared.

Rebecca wrung her sweating hands together, a feeling of desolation swamping her as he shoved open the door and they moved slowly inside the chilled room. A musty smell assaulted her, the scent of decay, rotting wood and mold mingling with the smell of despair. This place reeked of sadness, desertion, death.

Her son's?

Wind whistled through the weathered boards, and spiderwebs dangled from the ceilings and corners. A child's broken bat and a worn glove lay on the floor in one of the bedrooms, the faded chenille bedspread pilled and stained with what looked like blood. She sighed in relief when she realized the blood was dried and crusted and such a dark brown that it couldn't be fresh.

Ethan used a penlight from his pocket and swung it across the room, but what little furniture that had been there was now sagging with age, and as they inched through the five-room cottage, she knew their trip had been futile.

Jesse was not inside.

And neither was Finn. If he had brought Jesse here, they were long gone.

Tears choked her. They were never going to find Jesse.

Chapter Fifteen

Finn parked at the shipyard, his pulse racing at the thought of finally finishing his phase of the mission. He'd worked months setting his plan into motion, insinuating himself into Rebecca and Jesse's life, planting bugs in their houses, installing cameras, keeping tabs on Ethan Matalon. The memory of watching Rebecca on camera rolled through his head and his body hardened. He'd enjoyed the show, had pleasured himself as she'd undressed in the dim light of her bedroom, showered beneath the camera, curled up in the bed alone.

Playing with Matalon's head the past few hours had been the icing on the cake.

What would he do when he and his father and brothers finally completed the plan?

A sense of disappointment threatened to consume him. They hadn't discussed anything beyond the mission, beyond the sweet taste of revenge. Beyond the end of the men who'd betrayed them.

Spurned by renewed anger and restless energy, Finn climbed from the truck, circled to the back and raised the door to the bed of the utility truck. Around him, the air stirred with the smell of the river, the sweat of workers who helped build the ships, the scent of hard labor.

Finn shone a flashlight inside the truck, saw the boy hovering in the corner. He climbed up to get him, but suddenly Jesse vaulted from the corner, dropped to the ground and broke into a run.

Finn leaped down, grabbed him by the shirt and picked him up, but the boy pummeled him with his fists and kicked at his stomach. Dammit, he'd known the boy was a handful, but he'd expected him to be too scared to fight him. He should have drugged him.

Jesse's small fist slammed into Finn's eye with such force that he cursed and tightened his hold.

"Stop it, kid, or you won't ever see your parents again."

"You're not taking me to them anyway!" Jesse cried, kicking harder.

Finn shoved the boy back down inside the truck, and slapped a hand over his mouth. "I was getting ready to call them, but if you want me to put you in that river first, I will."

That shut the kid up fast.

Jesse glared at him with eyes bright with tears, but he didn't let them fall. Finn had to admit he admired the boy. If he had a child, he'd want him to be like Jesse.

Stop it. You can't think about him like that, or you won't be able to kill him.

And he had to kill him. That was the best way to make Matalon pay.

He retrieved his cell phone from his pocket and punched in Ethan's number. Time for the grand finale.

JESSE DIDN'T TRUST MR. FRANK. He was nothing like he used to be when he coached the team.

His voice was as cold as ice. His eyes had turned beady, and that vein in his forehead kept jumping up and down. But why was he so mad? Why had he hurt him and kept him away from his parents? Did he want money from Jesse's daddy?

That didn't make sense. Mr. Frank drove a big fancy car back in L.A. He always seemed to have plenty of money.

Mr. Frank frowned at him, and Jesse knew he had to figure out how to escape, that Mr. Frank was never going to let him go.

While Mr. Frank punched in numbers on his phone, Jesse stared over his shoulder, trying to figure out where he was. It was so dark it was hard to tell, but it looked like a marina.

But where? Boston was one big harbor. Boats and ships and water everywhere. His chin quivered. He wanted to be brave like his daddy, wanted to figure out how to sneak away. But all the boats and docks looked the same.

He needed to find a sign or some landmark to guide him.

Sucking back tears, he searched the dock

for people. If someone walked by or was near enough, he could yell for help. But the place was deserted.

Some big buildings that looked like warehouses sat to the right. He saw ships in between, and machines—big heavy cranes and moving equipment.

Machines meant they were building something here.

He strained his ears to listen to the sounds around him. The ocean? A boat sputtering? Cruise ships?

But the blackout must have stopped the boats from coming in and out. And the water…it wasn't choppy like the ocean but quiet. Maybe they were on one of the rivers.

Then Jesse saw a sign. Fore River. The ships…the machines… He knew where he was. He just had to find a way to let his daddy know so he could come and get him.

ETHAN FELT NUMB AS HE maneuvered the boat back into the harbor. He'd hoped beyond hope that Finn would be at the cottage.

What now?

He didn't have another lead, no place to look. Or rather, too many damn places.

His cell phone trilled. Silently willing the caller to be Finn, or Ty with news that he'd located Jesse, he yanked it up and checked the number. Out Of Area.

Rebecca clasped her hands as if praying or trying to physically hold herself together.

"Ethan Matalon."

"How does it feel to lose everything?"

Finn Shea's low, vile voice sent Ethan's heart racing. "If you want revenge, Shea, then come and get me. I'm tired of your damn games."

He disconnected the phone with a curse, then winced as Rebecca's mouth gaped open in horrified shock.

"Ethan, what are you doing?"

"He'll call back," Ethan said, pent-up fury hardening his voice. "It's no fun if we don't have a confrontation. And if I have to push it, I will."

"But what about Jesse?" Rebecca cried. She grabbed his arm and sent the boat swaying. "What if you make him so mad he kills him?"

"You mean if he hasn't already?" Ethan snarled.

The silence that stretched between them rattled with fear and doubt.

"You think our son is dead?" Rebecca whispered.

He had no idea, but they couldn't go on like this.

Rebecca stared at his phone, and he squeezed it, praying it would ring. But as they climbed from the boat and headed to his car, the daunting silence echoed in his ears, shrill and whispering that Finn wouldn't call back, that he might have misjudged Finn, that Finn would make Ethan suffer for hanging up on him.

REBECCA SHOOK AS SHE GOT inside Ethan's car. How could he have hung up on Finn? What if he'd called to make a deal? To tell them Jesse was all right?

Now they might never know.

Her phone jangled, and she snatched it up and glared at Ethan. "Hello."

"Your husband has a temper," Finn said in

a menacing voice. "He's going to get Jesse killed, or doesn't he care about the boy?"

"Is Jesse alive?" Rebecca asked. "Tell me. What have you done with him?"

"Did you find my cameras?" he asked, taunting her.

"Yes, you sick bastard. Now, if my son is alive, let me speak to him."

"Why should I do that?"

"Please, Frank," Rebecca pleaded softly. "He's just a little boy."

"My name is Finn."

"But Jesse liked you and trusted you. On some level, you must care about him."

"What I care about is my father and getting justice for him."

"Then stop this madness, because hurting an innocent child is not justice," Rebecca pleaded. "It's cruel and inhuman. Jesse has nothing to do with this."

"Ethan has to know what it's like to lose his family," Finn snarled, "just like I did when he betrayed my father."

"I'm his family, too, Finn. Take me and

release Jesse. We'll make a trade. Just let me know Jesse's all right."

Ethan was shaking his head no, but Rebecca ignored him. "Please, I'm begging you. Let me talk to him."

A heartbeat of silence, then a small sound.

"Mommy?"

"Jesse!" Rebecca choked on tears. Dear God, he was alive. Ethan's eyes darkened with emotions as he leaned forward to listen.

"Jesse, honey, we miss you so much," Rebecca whispered. "Are you okay?"

"I wanna come home, Mommy."

"I know, sweetheart. Daddy and I are going to get you."

"I'm here, son," Ethan said in a gravelly voice. "Tell me where you are."

Finn's cold voice reverberated in the background, although Rebecca couldn't make out what he was saying.

"I wanna come back and finish our model, Daddy," Jesse whispered.

Ethan's jaw tightened. "We will, Jesse—"

"That's enough," Finn said as he snatched

the phone back from Jesse. "Now, Matalon, you have less than an hour to find us."

Ethan jerked the phone from Rebecca's hand. "Tell me where to meet you," Ethan snapped.

"Your son just told you," Finn said with a nasty chuckle.

Then the phone clicked into silence.

Ethan sat stunned, looking perplexed.

"Where are they?" Rebecca asked.

"I'm not sure."

"What did Jesse say?" Rebecca jerked his hands. "Think, Ethan."

"He wanted to finish our model."

"The model of the ship," Rebecca said, remembering the one she'd seen on his home desk. "Could Finn have taken him back to your place?"

"We'll check, but there may be another possibility."

She clutched him, desperate, knowing they had to hurry. "What?"

"Ty and I were talking about the ports, about a possible terrorist attack, how easy it would be to escape on one of the ships. Jesse mentioned the shipbuilding… Maybe for a reason? Maybe Finn has Jesse at Fore River—that's where they build ships."

Rebecca clutched the seat edge, and Ethan started the engine and sped toward his house. They'd check there first, then go to the shipyard at the river.

She closed her eyes, latched on to the sound of Jesse's voice. He was alive, that was all that mattered. They still had a chance to rescue him.

IT WAS TIME FOR THE SHOWDOWN. The fact that Finn would have chosen the shipbuilding port made perfect sense. He'd seen the models in Ethan's home, knew he and Jesse built them together. It was just the kind of personal detail Finn would notice.

His house was on the way so he stopped there first but found it empty. But he grabbed extra ammunition for his gun, strapped a knife around one ankle and a small pistol around the other.

Rebecca watched quietly, her movements jittery with nerves.

He turned and pulled her to him. She wasn't going to like it but he didn't intend to take her with him. "I want you to stay here, Bec."

"No." Rebecca jutted her chin up in determination. "I'm going with you."

He cupped her face in his hands. "Listen to me, it's too dangerous. I need to focus on finding Jesse and getting him out safely, not worry about you being hurt."

She clenched his arms in a white-knuckled grip. "Ethan, you are not leaving me here alone. I have to be there. Jesse needs me."

He lowered his voice, his heart spasming. "I'll bring him home to you, Bec. I promise."

Her eyes beseeched him. "But, Ethan, I know Finn as Frank Sullivan. I saw him with those boys when he coached, saw another side of him. Maybe I can appeal to that side, reach him on some level."

"I told you it's too dangerous," Ethan snapped.

Rebecca flinched, then anger darkened her eyes. "So you're going to go charging off to rescue him alone just like you do on your secret missions. Is that the way it will be when we get him back, Ethan? You'll shut me out or leave us again?"

The uncertainty and bitterness lacing her voice tore at him. And the thought of something happening to her, of losing her permanently, terrified him.

"Dammit, I love you, Rebecca. You're the mother of my son, and I'm trying to protect you." His voice cracked. "If something happens to me, I want you alive to take care of Jesse."

Fear and a half dozen other emotions glittered in her eyes. "Nothing is going to happen to you," she said emphatically. "And this is one battle we're going to fight together, Ethan."

She jerked away from him and headed to the door, then swung it open.

"Rebecca, please."

"Come on, Ethan. We're wasting time."

He sighed and followed her to the car. He had never seen Rebecca look so determined, so driven.

Then again, their son had never been in danger before.

And she was right. Time was running out. They couldn't waste another minute.

FINN SHOVED JESSE ONTO THE deck of the container ship, his adrenaline pumping. Ethan would be here soon.

And Finn would finally get to feel his blood on his hands. His phone buzzed, and he checked the number on the display scene.

His father.

"Hello, Dad."

"Is it done?"

"Almost. Matalon's on the way."

"Good. Finish them up, then meet me at the designated location."

Finn grinned and imagined the fireworks display yet to come. Boston had been steeped in darkness now for an entire day.

But soon, when the bomb was detonated, the sky would light up the emptiness. And when the people of Boston awoke, they would feel its effects, and know that their own vice-president, the man they'd elected—instead of his father—to serve them, was the cause of it.

Chapter Sixteen

As Ethan approached the shipyard, his anxiety intensified. He wished Rebecca had listened and stayed at home. But she'd always had a mind of her own, and her fierce love for Jesse had turned her into a mother bear protecting her cub.

He also had the sneaking suspicion that she wanted to confront Finn Shea herself, that she still harbored guilt for allowing Frank Sullivan to fool her.

Finn would pay for that, as well as for the torture he'd inflicted upon all of them today. The memory of finding Jesse's blood in the car trunk and his cap in that condo explosion still haunted him. How badly was Jesse hurt?

Rolling his shoulders to alleviate the

tension, he latched on to the sound of Jesse's voice when Finn had phoned. Jesse was alive and would be all right. Ethan would take him and Rebecca home and never let anyone hurt them again.

The car bounced over a rut in the curvy road, then he spotted the sign for Fore River and the shipyard ahead, so he turned into the entrance, weaving between the massive buildings. Vessel and cargo containers loomed like a maze with cranes and heavy machinery interspersed through the layout. Normally the sound of work crews, machines and construction would fill the air, but the blackout had ceased production today just as it had other businesses in Boston.

Jesse could be on any one of the ships, hidden away in the dark, locked in a hold below deck or inside one of the cargo containers.

How in the hell was he going to find him?

"This place is huge." Rebecca's voice carried the same overwhelming doubt that gnawed at him. "Where do we start?"

Ethan scrubbed a hand over his mouth, studying the layout, trying to think. In his research, he hadn't discovered anything about Finn or the Sheas sharing ownership or stock in any businesses that might use the cargo ships. Or had he?

He had to think like Finn.

Tension knotted his body as he reached for the door handle. "Stay here, Rebecca. Let me search the containers."

Rebecca opened her car door. "No, Ethan. We're doing this together."

She jumped out of the car before he could stop her, then tilted her head and searched the darkness.

Suddenly a shot pinged through the air and whizzed past her head.

"Get down!" Ethan shouted.

She ducked, squatting down behind the passenger side of the car to shield herself.

Another bullet hit the windshield of the car, shattering the glass, and a third one soared toward Ethan, lodging into the car door within an inch of him.

He hunkered down beside the car and scanned the distance, trying to see where the shots were coming from.

He had no doubt the identity of the shooter. Finn Shea.

He had set a trap for them by using Jesse. He wanted a showdown.

And Ethan would give him one. But Finn would not walk away alive.

REBECCA'S HEART POUNDED AS SHE crouched beside Ethan. She had always had this vision of what marriage and family should be like. She guessed it stemmed from her parents' marriage—a mom who'd stayed home, a father who'd provided. She had wanted a career, though, and had fallen short of her own expectations when they'd first been married.

Ethan had fallen short of the image she'd had for him, too.

But he was not falling short now. He would do anything for their son, even sacrifice his own life.

"I'm going after him, Bec. Stay here."

"No way."

He inched forward, then ran to duck behind a truck. She followed behind, keeping low and close on his heels.

Another shot pinged, bouncing off the hood of the truck.

"Where is he?" Rebecca whispered.

Ethan's eyebrows were drawn in concentration as he scanned the mammoth-size steel vessels and passageways between the buildings.

He pointed toward the left, to several ships docked at the edge of the river. "The shots are coming from that direction."

"Which container?"

"I don't know yet. Keep watching."

Something caught her attention in the distance. A small pinpoint of light.

Her pulse raced as she recognized the source, and she tugged Ethan's arm. "Ethan, look over there. It's Jesse, I know it is. He's trying to signal us."

He pivoted, searching. "What makes you think that?"

"That light," Rebecca said, excitement budding in her chest.

"Where?" Ethan asked. "It looks like a firefly."

"It's the neon wand I bought Jesse at the Red Sox game. He has it with him."

Ethan frowned but turned back and angled his head in the direction she indicated. She saw the moment he realized she might be right.

A narrow point of light flickered from the black recesses of the dock on a vessel closest to one of the cranes where a small motor boat was tied to the side.

The motorboat—Finn's transportation out of there.

"He's holding Jesse on that ship," Rebecca whispered. "And he has his motorboat ready to go so he can escape."

"Finn won't get away this time." Ethan grabbed her hand, and together they ran toward the ship, weaving in and out of the passageways between the containers and warehouses, ducking behind trucks and huge drums as Finn continued to fire.

ETHAN CLUTCHED REBECCA'S HAND pulling her along behind him as he darted in between the heavy cranes and trucks, using his body as a human shield to protect her. A loading dock to the left provided cover as they ran toward the ship where Finn held Jesse. Ethan kept his eyes trained on the small light, letting it guide him as it flickered against the darkness.

But as they neared the ship and began to climb aboard from the side, Finn fired again. Ethan threw himself over Rebecca to protect her, but the bullet grazed his arm. He ignored it then saw a shadow moving to the right. The neon wand moved as well, telling him Finn was on the run.

Ethan crawled onto the deck, helped Rebecca up, then squatted down low and followed the shadow across the deck, grimacing as he spotted Finn's hand shoving Jesse along.

"Finn, stop now!" Ethan shouted.

Finn spun around and fired, and Ethan jumped sideways to avoid the bullet.

"Daddy!" Jesse screamed.

A second later, Finn pushed Jesse down the steps toward the holds. Ethan turned to make sure Rebecca hadn't been hit, then motioned to her, indicating that he was going to follow Finn.

She nodded, and he removed his gun and braced it with his left hand, ready to fire as they silently edged forward. Step by step, they inched down the stairwell and through the narrow passageways to the holds where the cargo containers were stowed.

Another maze hid Finn from view, slowing Ethan as he rounded each storage container and braced for gunfire. Ahead, to the right, footsteps pounded, then the flash of the wand sparkled again, so he veered around another container, following the trail.

Finn was leading them below so he could kill them, then stick them in one of the containers. The ship would move out without anyone realizing there were dead bodies on board, giving Finn plenty of time to cover himself and escape.

He considered sending Rebecca back up on deck to call for help but didn't want to chance Finn nabbing her during their separation.

"Finn, stop being a coward and show yourself!" Ethan shouted.

"Please, Frank," Rebecca cried. "Let us have Jesse back."

Ethan squeezed her hand, and they took another step forward, then Finn must have decided he'd led them deep enough into the bowels of the holds that he was ready for the confrontation, because he stepped from the shadows with Jesse in front of him, a Glock pointed at Jesse's head.

Jesse looked up at him with frightened, big brown eyes. Eyes that searched his father's for answers. Eyes that flicked sideways toward his captor.

Eyes that trusted Ethan to save him.

Fear pressed against Ethan's chest, cutting off his breath. He had to live up to that trust.

Behind him, Rebecca released a terrorized sob. He squeezed her hand again, silently offering comfort and willing her to remain calm.

"Please, Frank," Rebecca said softly, calling him by the name he'd used when he'd tried to seduce her. "Let Jesse go. He's just an innocent little boy."

"I'm Finn, so stop calling me Frank." His hatred-filled look speared Ethan with accusations. Jesse struggled to free himself, but Finn tightened his hand on his small shoulder, holding him in place. Jesse winced in pain.

Finn merely smiled. "This boy needs to know the truth about his father."

"What truth is that?" Rebecca asked. "That he loves him? That Ethan is a hero, not like you, a monster who hurts children? That Ethan would do anything for his son?"

Finn's jaw clenched in anger. "That Ethan betrayed my father. That my father spent ten years in jail because Ethan and the others let him down. They should have stood up for my father, told the truth, that the mission went awry because of Grant Davis, that it wasn't my father's fault people died that day, that my father was set up." Finn's voice grew louder in agitation. "That my father should be sitting in the White House, not Davis."

"If you have proof of that, then you and Liam should have taken it to the courts, not set out to exact your own revenge," Ethan said in a lethally calm voice.

"My family suffered because of you and the others, because you were all cowards."

"My daddy isn't a coward!" Jesse yelled. "He's smart and brave and nicer than you!"

Suddenly Jesse jerked around and bit Finn on the hand. Finn howled and momentarily dropped his gun hand, while Jesse started to run. Ethan raised his gun toward Finn, ready to fire, and Rebecca threw herself in front of Jesse and pushed him behind her, protecting him with her body.

Finn lurched forward, raised his gun, and aimed it at Jesse and Rebecca. Ethan couldn't get a shot off for fear he'd hit them, so he dove toward Finn, grabbed his gun hand and swung it upward, then body-slammed Finn's chest, knocking them both to the ground. The gun went off, sending a bullet flying.

"Run, Rebecca!" Ethan shouted. "Get Jesse out of here."

Finn's gun dislodged another round, sending a bullet into one of the containers. Ethan karate-chopped Finn's wrist, and Finn dropped the weapon with a howl. Cursing, Finn tried to retrieve the gun, but Ethan kicked it and sent the Glock skidding across the floor. Finn managed to punch

Ethan in the stomach, then raised his fist and swung toward Ethan's face, but Ethan turned sideways to dodge the blow. He jerked to a standing position and saw Rebecca grab Jesse and run behind one of the containers.

Sweat poured from Ethan's face and soaked his shirt as he slammed into Finn again and again. Finn cursed, then kicked upward in a martial arts move. Ethan deftly dodged the move, then spun around and slammed his foot into Finn's face with a swift kick. Finn staggered and collapsed onto his knees, spitting blood and cursing.

But he recovered quickly and came at Ethan like a wild animal. They traded blow for blow, fists pounding flesh, their anger driving them with vicious blows.

Shaking with fury, Ethan managed to wrap his hands around Finn's throat and began to squeeze. He wanted to choke him, watch the life drain away, feel him take his last breath.

"Daddy!" Jesse cried, his voice filled with terror and shock. Vaguely, he realized that Rebecca was trying to coax Jesse toward the stairs to climb on deck, but Jesse refused to leave Ethan.

Finn coughed and tried to tear Ethan's hands from his throat, but Ethan tightened his fingers, digging into the man's larynx. Every agonizing second since Jesse's abduction flashed back. The anguish and fear in Rebecca's eyes. The gut-wrenching grief he and Rebecca had both experienced when they'd seen that condo explode and thought Jesse had died inside. The heart-pounding terror when he'd seen Finn holding that gun to his son's head.

Rage vibrated in every muscle in Ethan's body, in his soul. A rage like nothing he'd ever felt before.

"Go ahead, kill me." Finn's eyes glittered with challenge and contempt. "Let your son see you for what you are. A bastard and a murderer."

Ethan gripped him even tighter, shaking him with pent-up fury. But Finn's goading cut through that rage like a knife.

His son had defended him in front of Finn. His son thought he was brave, a nicer man than Finn, that he represented honor and justice and goodness.

Even with hatred eating at him, could he traumatize his son by making him watch his father kill a man in cold blood?

Chapter Seventeen

Finn had known going into this that he might die. But he was willing to give up his life to get the revenge he craved and the justice his father deserved.

Turning Matalon into a killer in front of his own kid was not the ending he'd first envisioned, but if he didn't survive, he would have still won. The boy would be changed forever, and Ethan would be exposed to his wife and child as a killer, not a hero.

Still, Finn didn't intend to die.

Instead, he faked it. He shuddered and closed his eyes as if struggling for air, dropped his hands so they hung limply by his side.

His words must have triggered Matalon's integrity, though, because Ethan suddenly released Finn and shoved him to the floor. Matalon was reaching for something to tie him up, but Finn took advantage of that split second, grabbed the knife inside his pocket, flipped it open and stabbed Ethan's thigh.

Caught off guard, Ethan yelped and twisted around to fight him, but Finn flipped his body sideways, grabbed his gun and fired.

The bullet pierced Ethan in the shoulder, and he dropped to his knees, staggering to drag himself back upright.

Rebecca screamed and darted from behind the container, pushing Jesse in front of her toward the steps leading to the deck.

Finn heaved for a breath, then slammed his foot into Ethan's face. Blood spurted from Ethan's nose and mouth, then he groaned and collapsed.

Finn couldn't let Rebecca escape, not with the boy. They'd talk.

Finn didn't intend to end up in jail.

He would be back for Matalon and finish him off. For now, he'd let him lie in his own blood. Then he'd bring Rebecca and the boy back, wake him up and kill them in front of him.

To cover his ass, he'd stuff them all in one of the containers and head out to help his father finish off Grant Davis.

REBECCA BIT BACK A SOB AS SHE pushed Jesse through the maze of containers. She hated to leave Ethan, but she had to get Jesse to safety. Ethan would want that, too.

Was he still alive? Would he survive?

"Mommy?"

"Shh, we have to get out of here."

Jesse balked. "But we can't leave Daddy!"

She knelt and cupped his face with her hands. "We have to get help, Jesse. You understand? We're not leaving Daddy, we're going to find help for him. He needs a doctor."

His tears dampened her palms, but he nodded. Dammit, all she wanted to do was hold her son and comfort him. She didn't want to leave Ethan, either. But she was unarmed, had no way to fight Finn alone.

Footsteps clattered on the cement floor

behind her, and panic squeezed her chest. "Go, Jesse. Hurry!"

Jesse ran forward and veered to the left. She raced behind him, but it was so dark she couldn't see in front of her, and she couldn't remember where the stairs were located. She and Ethan had woven through the maze, and she was lost, trapped in the corner.

"You can't escape, Rebecca." Finn's menacing tone sent a chill down her spine. "Matalon is dead, and you're mine now."

No, Ethan wasn't dead. He couldn't be.

"Mommy?"

"Go, Jesse, go. If he gets me, you keep running, go toward the street, find help somewhere."

His body trembled beneath her hand, and she squeezed his shoulder. They came to a staircase but instead of leading up toward the deck, it went down. Finn's footsteps grew closer. There was no place else to run.

She led Jesse down the stairs, feeling her way through the dark. The passageways were narrow, the space hot, loud with the sound of pipes rumbling. Jesse flipped on the neon wand, and she realized they were in the boiler room.

She hurried on, pulling Jesse around the pipes, hoping to find an exit on the other side. Finn's footsteps clanged on the steps. He was turning the corner, growing closer.

She dragged Jesse behind a steel beam behind some pipes. "Switch off the light," she whispered.

He shuddered but bravely obeyed her command, pitching them in a black cavern of emptiness. She clung to him, willing him to be strong. The footsteps paused on the steps, hesitated then moved again.

She held her breath as Finn walked across the room. Jesse buried his head in her arms, shrinking back as far into the corner as possible.

"Rebecca, Jesse, where are you?" Finn sang.

She shuddered at the sound of his taunting. How could she ever have thought the man was nice? That he cared for her or Jesse?

Jesse burrowed against her, and she stroked his back, covering her mouth with one hand to keep from crying as the shadow of Finn's hulking body loomed in front of them. He walked past their hiding spot, searching, almost humming, calling their names over and over.

A tense minute passed, then another. His choppy breathing rattled in the quiet. The smell of his sweat and evil soul permeated the air.

Then she heard him heading past her. Crossing the room to the opposite side. He must have thought she'd found the exit and made it through.

Releasing a pent-up breath, she tugged Jesse's hand, and they inched out from their hiding spot and tiptoed back toward the door they'd entered.

But just as she found the first step, she sensed something behind her. In that split second Finn yanked her by the hair and dragged her up against him. His vile breath bathed her cheek as he pressed the cold barrel of the gun to her temple.

"Make any sudden moves and you and the boy die right here," Finn growled.

Rebecca whimpered but did as he ordered as he shoved her and Jesse up the metal stairs, back to the spot where Ethan lay dying.

PAIN CLAWED AT ETHAN'S LEG, arm and shoulder, but he roused himself from unconsciousness. His head was spinning like a freaking top, and his limbs ached with fatigue and blood loss, but he had to save Jesse and Rebecca. He reached a hand inside his pocket, retrieved a handkerchief and pressed it inside his shirt to absorb the blood from the shoulder wound. A sharp pain splintered his thigh as he dragged himself up to stand, and he swayed, grabbing the edge of one of the containers to steady himself. Fear pounded in his chest as he listened for sounds of Rebecca and Jesse.

Had they gotten away?

Or had Finn found them?

He blinked against the darkness, trying to orient himself, to find his gun, then footsteps pounded on the steps leading from below. No time to find his weapon.

Moving on autopilot, he maneuvered between the containers, hiding behind one as the footsteps grew louder. Seconds later, he squinted through the shadows and saw Jesse appear, followed by Rebecca and Finn.

His heart stopped in his chest. Finn had his

gun pressed against Rebecca's temple. Any sudden move and the gun might dislodge, and Rebecca would be dead.

Sweat beaded on his brow and rolled down the sides of his face. He held his breath while he waited for them to clear the stairs, then Finn pushed Rebecca back toward where he'd left Ethan. Ethan lunged from behind the container and grabbed Finn around the neck in a chokehold.

"Drop the weapon, Finn."

Finn lowered the gun slightly, and Ethan yelled at Rebecca to run. She grabbed Jesse and raced through the maze of containers toward the steps leading to the upper deck.

Ethan tightened his hold on Finn and ordered him again to drop the gun to the floor, but Finn growled and kicked backward into Ethan's wounded thigh. Ethan buckled in pain. That split second provided Finn with just enough time to escape. As he charged after Rebecca, he fired again at Ethan, but Ethan dodged the bullet.

Ethan clawed his way up the steps and spotted Finn. He'd caught up with Rebecca and Jesse and was shoving them off the ship into the small speedboat.

Ethan ran across the deck, jumped off and headed toward another boat tied to the dock. Finn had already started the engine and sped into the channel.

Ethan started the second boat and tore through the water after him. Finn turned and fired, and Ethan ducked. Water sprayed and pummeled him as he cut through the choppy waves created by the wake of Finn's boat. He accelerated, slowly gaining on Finn, steering sideways in a zigzag pattern to avoid his repeated shots. Rebecca pushed Jesse to the floor, covering him with her body to protect him. Ethan wanted to fire but couldn't take a chance on a stray bullet catching one of them.

Pain ripped through Ethan as the boat bounced over the waves. He wished he'd killed the bastard when he'd had the chance. If anything happened to Rebecca or his son…

Ahead a larger ship appeared, and Finn spun around the opposite way to avoid a collision, forcing Ethan to do the same. Seconds later, he closed the distance to Finn.

Finn fired again, then slammed the gun down. Had he used his last bullet? Ethan maneuvered the boat alongside Finn's, then lunged over the edge of his boat and vaulted onto Finn, knocking him down. The boat Ethan had been driving shot forward, slamming into the dock and exploding.

Ethan pounded Finn with his fists while the boat raced toward the fiery blaze.

Rebecca jumped up, grabbed the steering wheel and swung the boat to the left, slowing the speed and missing the burning boat.

"You'll never win," Finn snarled. "And you won't stop my father."

"Yes, we will." Rage overpowered Ethan. He slammed his fist into Finn's face, this time punching him so hard that Finn's head hit the bottom of the boat with a sickening thud.

His body jerked, blood trickled from his nose, then he went still and faded into unconsciousness.

"Daddy!" Jesse cried.

Ethan glanced sideways, then pulled his

son into his arms as Rebecca slowed the boat and guided it up to the dock.

Ethan never wanted to let Jesse go. It felt heavenly to have him in his arms, but he couldn't take the chance of Finn waking up and surprising him again. So he hugged Jesse fiercely, told him he loved him, then gently handed him to Rebecca. Then he quickly grabbed some rope from the boat and tied Finn's wrists and ankles.

Rebecca fell into his arms, shaking and bringing Jesse with her. He clutched them both, breathing hard and planting kisses all over both of their faces. "God, I'm so glad to have you two back," he whispered hoarsely.

"I was scared," Jesse admitted.

"We were scared, too." Rebecca rubbed his back and hugged him between them. "But you were so brave, sweetheart. Daddy and I are proud of you."

"We sure are, buddy," Ethan murmured. "You kept your cool, and you even told me where to look for you."

"And you helped us find you with that neon wand," Rebecca said, choking on tears.

Ethan scooped up Jesse with his good arm, and the three of them huddled together for a tender moment.

"We have to get you to a doctor," Rebecca said in a low voice. "You need medical attention, Ethan."

"Soon," he said softly, although his energy was draining. "For now, I just want to hold both of you."

She kissed him, then pressed a hand to his chest, but concern darkened her eyes when she felt the blood dampening his shirt. "Ethan, come on. We've been through too much together tonight to lose you now."

His gaze met hers, understanding and love binding them together. The past few hours had been harrowing. At times he'd had no idea if they'd make it out alive or if they'd ever find their son, but with each awful moment that had passed, one thing had become clearer and clearer. He loved Rebecca and his son and wanted them to be a family again. And this time he'd do whatever it took to make their relationship work.

"Ethan, please, let's get you to the doctor."

He nodded. Knowing he needed to get Finn into custody, Ethan finally released his fierce hold on her and Jesse. But he silently thanked God for bringing his family back together again. He helped them off the boat, then he called Ty to fill him in on what had happened and have Finn picked up and taken into custody.

Just as the port authority and the police arrived, Ethan lost the battle and faded into unconsciousness.

Chapter Eighteen

Wrapped in a blanket, Rebecca huddled with Jesse in the waiting room of the hospital. Paralyzed with fear, she felt the minutes slowly tick by. The paramedics had said Ethan's injuries weren't life-threatening. But he had lost blood, and, after today's events, Rebecca couldn't shake the fear that she still might lose him.

She clutched Jesse tighter, rocking him back and forth in her arms just as she'd done when he was a baby. Normally, he wouldn't tolerate such behavior, but he had been worried about his father when they'd taken him into surgery, and he was exhausted.

"Mommy?"

She feathered his soft blond hair from his face, and stared into his big brown eyes. Eyes so like his father's. She loved them both so much she hurt. "What, sweetheart?"

"Daddy is going to be okay, isn't he?"

"Yes, honey. But the doctor had to remove the bullet from his shoulder." Thank goodness the hospital had backup generators.

His eyelids lowered, and he yawned. He was fighting so hard to stay awake, just as he'd fought so hard to be brave. "Do we have to go back to L.A. now?"

Her heart clenched. She didn't know how to answer him, didn't know for sure what Ethan wanted.

But she knew she couldn't leave him tonight or tomorrow. Not until he was better…

Or even then.

She wanted to be with him forever. But she'd take whatever time he had to offer.

"No, we're not leaving for a while," she said softly. "We have to stay here and take care of Daddy."

"Good. I don't want to go back to L.A.," Jesse said in a hoarse whisper.

She smiled and rocked him against her. "I know, sweetheart. Neither do I. Now, go to sleep. I'll wake you up when Daddy comes out of surgery."

His big eyes beseeched hers, still filled with trauma. "Promise?"

"I promise."

He finally gave into fatigue, closed his eyes and fell asleep, his breathing growing shallow and low in a peaceful rhythm.

Ty approached her bearing coffee, and she accepted it gratefully.

"Are you all right?" he asked.

She nodded and took a long look at her sleeping son, so grateful he was back safe in her arms that tears filled her eyes again. She'd never get tired of looking at him.

"Yes, Ty. Thank you for all you did to help us."

Ty shrugged. "Ethan's my friend. And he loves you. You know that, don't you?"

She smiled and sipped the coffee. "I know, but it wasn't enough before." She just hoped it would be this time.

Ty's phone rang, and he excused himself to answer it, a tense expression drawing his eyebrows together as he listened.

The doctor approached, frowning over bifocals and sending her heart sputtering again.

"Is Ethan all right?" she asked frantically.

"Mr. Matalon is awake but groggy. Follow me, and I'll take you to him."

She wrapped the blanket around Jesse and carried him as she followed the doctor to the hospital room.

"I told him he should stay overnight," the doctor said as he pushed open the door, "but he's insisting on going home."

"That sounds like Ethan," she said, smiling as she entered the room. Ethan was trying to sit up, pushing his legs over to the side.

"Let's get out of here, Bec."

"Ethan, wait a minute. Just lie back and let's talk," she said softly.

He muttered a sigh of frustration but did as she requested. Jesse stirred and Ethan reached for him. She settled him onto the bed on Ethan's uninjured side.

"Watch your shoulder," Rebecca warned.

"Daddy?" Jesse smiled and cuddled next to his father.

"I'm okay, son. We're all okay now that

we're together," Ethan said gruffly. He glanced at Rebecca. "And we'll be better when we get home."

"We'll stay here with you tonight," Rebecca said.

His gaze met hers, darkening with emotion. "I want to be home with you and our son. This day's been too hard for us to end up here."

"But you need your rest," Rebecca insisted.

He cleared his throat. "So do you, Bec."

"Get the discharge papers ready, Doc," Ethan said.

The doctor shook his head but agreed, then excused himself. Ethan pulled her hand in his, urging her to sit beside him on the bed, then pressed a hand to her cheek. "This bed isn't big enough for all of us."

"Ethan, stay here, sweetheart. Let the doctors take care of you."

"No. I want Jesse in his own room, and I want you in my bed tonight."

"Just tonight?" she whispered.

He shook his head, and saw tears glitter in his brown eyes. "Tonight and every night afterward." He cleared his throat, tucked her hair behind her ear. "I messed up before when I let you go. And tonight when I thought I might lose Jesse, and then you… God, I never want to feel that desperate fear again. If something had happened to you, I couldn't have gone on. I wouldn't have wanted to."

"Oh, Ethan." She brought her hands up and cradled his face between her palms. "I love you. It's always been you. And I want to be with you always."

"About our jobs…?" he said. "I've been thinking. I'll give up my Eclipse work, sell the company. I'll do anything to show you and Jesse how much I love you, how much I need you."

She pressed a kiss to his lips. "We'll talk about that later and work something out." She kissed him again. "Tonight let's just be together."

"Yes, I want that, too." He grabbed her arm so she could help him stand. "So take me home, sweetheart."

Bandaged and weak, tired and drained but

happy, the three of them returned to Ethan's brownstone as a family.

AS SOON AS ETHAN GOT SETTLED IN his bed at home and Rebecca had tucked Jesse safely in his bed, she curled up beside Ethan.

Ty, who had arrived shortly after them, approached them with a worried expression on his face. "I'm glad you guys are going to work things out. But I have to go, Ethan. The night isn't over yet."

Ethan's arm tightened around Rebecca's shoulders. "What's happened, Ty?"

"Grant Davis is still missing," Ty said. "And I just received word that Liam set a bomb somewhere in Boston. We have to find it before it goes off."

"How long do you have?" Ethan asked.

"No telling," Ty said grimly. "But the clock is ticking. If we don't find it, who knows how many people will die in this blackout."

* * * * *

*Turn the page for a sneak peek at the
conclusion of the* LIGHTS OUT *continuity,*
MEET ME AT MIDNIGHT
By Jessica Andersen
On sale in September
LIGHTS OUT:
Mystery and passion thrive in the dark...

Ty Jones paused in the shadows beyond a small, cobbled courtyard in Boston's North End, breathing past the tension of battle-readiness.

The light from a kerosene lantern broke the absolute darkness in the courtyard, casting warm shadows on the woman who waited for him in the hot, humid summer night. The lamplight should have been almost painfully romantic.

Instead, it was a necessity.

Boston had been in the grips of a wide-spread blackout for almost twenty-five hours now. Most of the city's inhabitants thought there had been a massive failure at Boston Light & Power, but Ty and his teammates knew that the blackout had been no accident—it had been a cover. Under the cloak of darkness, a man they'd once trusted had kidnapped Grant Davis, vice-president of the United States.

Now, twenty-five hours later, with Davis's life hanging in the balance and his captor hinting that a bomb had been planted somewhere in the city, Ty and the others were out of time and options.

Which had brought him here, to a clandestine rendezvous with Internet bombshell Gabriella Solaro.

Ty's watch chimed softly. It was ten o'clock. Time to meet the one connection they had left, the one woman who could possibly lead them to Liam Shea, the man behind the blackout.

Taking a deep breath, Ty stepped out of concealment and swung open the ornate wrought-iron gate that separated the North End courtyard from the narrow street. Pitching his voice low, he called, "Gabriella?"

The woman in the courtyard was facing away from him. At the sound of her name, she turned and lifted the lantern. "Tyler?"

Her voice was soft and feminine, just as he'd imagined it during their online conversations, first in a chat room at Webmatch.com, then one-on-one via e-mail and Instant Messenger. But, oddly, she looked nothing like he'd expected.

Her dark eyes complemented full, red-painted lips, and her features were sharp and exotic, but in the lantern light, her hair seemed darker than the fiery chestnut she'd mentioned, and her simple sundress made her seem more angular than her self-described curvy-bordering-on-plump.

She was lovely, but she wasn't anything like the picture in her profile. Then again, why should that surprise him? It was all too easy to bend the truth and become someone else on the Internet.

He should know.

Stepping forward, into the circle of lantern light, Ty hesitated, wondering what she'd expected. Should he hug her? Kiss her? They'd met through an online dating service, which carried a certain expectation, and they'd e-chatted long into many nights, forming the illusion of intimacy. But none of it had been real, had it?

More important, their last few exchanges had been increasingly tense, as he'd pressed for a meeting and she'd resisted, which had only solidified his suspicions even before Liam had made his move.

Now, though, he had a part to play. He leaned in and kissed her on the cheek. "It's nice to finally meet you in person."

If he hadn't been watching her face as he eased back, he would've missed the moment her eyes slid beyond him to a deeply shadowed corner where two brick-walled houses converged.

Instinct tightened the back of Ty's neck.

Someone was watching.

* * * * *

Welcome to cowboy country...

Turn the page for a sneak preview of
TEXAS BABY
by
Kathleen O'Brien
An exciting new title from
Harlequin Superromance
for everyone who loves
stories about the West.

Harlequin Superromance—
Where life and love weave together in
emotional and unforgettable ways.

CHAPTER ONE

CHASE TRANSFERRED his gaze to the road and identified a foreign spot on the horizon. A car. Almost half a mile away, where the straight, tree-lined drive met the public road. He could tell it was coming too fast, but judging the speed of a vehicle moving straight toward you was tricky.

It wasn't until it was about two hundred yards away that he realized the driver must be drunk...or crazy. Or both.

The guy was going maybe sixty. On a private drive, out here in ranch country, where kids or horses or tractors or stupid chickens might come darting out any minute, that was criminal. Chase straightened from his comfortable slouch and waved his hands.

"Slow down, you fool," he called out. He

took the porch steps quickly and began walking fast down the driveway.

The car veered oddly, from one lane to another, then up onto the slight rise of the thick green spring grass. It just barely missed the fence.

"Slow down, damn it!"

He couldn't see the driver, and he didn't recognize this automobile. It was small and old, and couldn't have cost much even when it was new. It was probably white, but now it needed either a wash or a new paint job or both.

"Damn it, what's wrong with you?"

At the last minute, he had to jump away, because the idiot behind the wheel clearly wasn't going to turn to avoid a collision. He couldn't believe it. The car kept coming, finally slowing a little, but it was too late.

Still going about thirty miles an hour, it slammed into the large, white-brick pillar that marked the front boundaries of the house. The pillar wasn't going to give an inch, so the car had to. The front end folded up like a paper fan.

It seemed to take forever for the car to

settle, as if the trauma happened in slow motion, reverberating from the front to the back of the car in ripples of destruction. The front windshield suddenly seemed to ice over with lethal bits of glassy frost. Then the side windows exploded.

The front driver's door wrenched open, as if the car wanted to expel its contents. Metal buckled hideously. Small pieces, like hubcaps and mirrors, skipped and ricocheted insanely across the oyster-shell driveway.

Finally, everything was still. Into the silence, a plume of steam shot up like a geyser, smelling of rust and heat. Its snake-like hiss almost smothered the low, agonized moan of the driver.

Chase's anger had disappeared. He didn't feel anything but a dull sense of disbelief. Things like this didn't happen in real life. Not in his life. Maybe the sun had actually put him to sleep....

But he was already kneeling beside the car. The driver was a woman. The frosty glass-ice of the windshield was dotted with small flecks of blood. She must have hit it with her head, because just below her hairline a red liquid was seeping out. He touched it. He tried to wipe it away before it reached her eyebrow, though, of course that made no sense at all. Her eyes were shut.

Was she conscious? Did he dare move her? Her dress was covered in glass, and the metal of the car was sticking out lethally in all the wrong places.

Then he remembered, with an intense relief, that every good medical man in the county was here, just behind the house, drinking his champagne. He found his phone and paged Trent.

The woman moaned again.

Alive, then. Thank God for that.

He saw Trent coming toward him, starting out at a lope, but quickly switching to a full run.

"Get Dr. Marchant," Chase called. "Don't bother with 911."

Trent didn't take long to assess the situation. A fraction of a second, and he began pulling out his cell phone and running toward the house.

The yelling seemed to have roused the woman. She opened her eyes. They were blue and clouded with pain and confusion.

"Chase," she said.

His breath stalled. His head pulled back. "What?"

Her only answer was another moan, and he wondered if he had imagined the word. He reached around her and put his arm behind her shoulders. She was tiny. Probably petite by nature, but surely way too thin. He could feel her shoulder blades pushing against her skin, as fragile as the wishbone in a turkey.

She seemed to have passed out, so he put his other arm under her knees and lifted her out. He tried to avoid the jagged metal, but her skirt caught on a piece and the tearing sound seemed to wake her again.

"No," she said. "Please."

"I'm just trying to help," he said. "It's going to be all right."

She seemed profoundly distressed. She wriggled in his arms, and she was so weak, like a broken bird. It made him feel too big and brutish. And intrusive. As if touching her this way, his bare hands against the warm skin behind her knees, were somehow a transgression.

He wished he could be more delicate. But he smelled gasoline, and he knew it wasn't safe to leave her here.

Finally he heard the sound of voices, as guests began to run around the side of the house, alerted by Trent. Dr. Marchant was at the front, racing toward them as if he were forty instead of seventy. Susannah was right behind him, her green dress floating around her trim legs.

"Please," the woman in his arms murmured again. She looked at him, the expression in her blue eyes lost and bewildered. He wondered if she might be on drugs. Hitting her head on the windshield might account for this unfocused, glazed look, but it couldn't explain the crazy driving.

"Please, put me down. Susannah… The wedding…"

Chase's arms tightened instinctively, and he froze in his tracks. She whimpered, and he realized he might be hurting her. "Say that again?"

"The wedding. I have to stop it."

＊＊＊＊＊

Be sure to look for TEXAS BABY,
available September 11, 2007,
as well as other fantastic
Superromance titles
available in September.

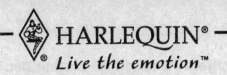

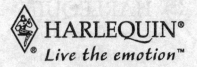

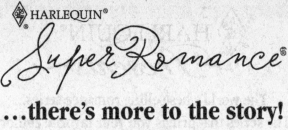

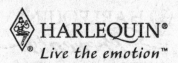

HARLEQUIN®
Presents~

The world's bestselling romance series...
The series that brings you your favorite authors,
month after month:

Helen Bianchin...Emma Darcy
Lynne Graham...Penny Jordan
Miranda Lee...Sandra Marton
Anne Mather...Carole Mortimer
Susan Napier...Michelle Reid

and many more uniquely talented authors!

Wealthy, powerful, gorgeous men...
Women who have feelings just like your own...
The stories you love, set in exotic, glamorous locations...

HARLEQUIN®
Presents~

Seduction and Passion Guaranteed!

Harlequin® Historical
Historical Romantic Adventure!

Imagine a time of chivalrous knights and unconventional ladies, roguish rakes and impetuous heiresses, rugged cowboys and spirited frontierswomen— these rich and vivid tales will capture your imagination!

Harlequin Historical . . . they're too good to miss!

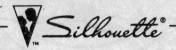

SPECIAL EDITION™

Emotional, compelling stories that capture the intensity of living, loving and creating a family in today's world.

Desire

Modern, passionate reads that are powerful and provocative.

nocturne

Dramatic and sensual tales of paranormal romance.

Romantic SUSPENSE

Romances that are sparked by danger and fueled by passion.